SnapShots

of

BELIZE

an anthology of short fiction

Leo Bradley
Zoila Ellis
Evadne Garcia
Evan X Hyde
Lawrence Vernon
Colville Young
John A. Watler

Edited by Michael D. Phillips

Published by Cubola Productions
35 Elizabeth Street
Benque Viejo del Carmen
Belize, C.A.

Printed and bound in Mexico

Design by A to Z Graphic Studio
Cover photograph by Esther Jurgens
Back cover photograph by Mina Bárcenas

First Edition, May 1995
Ninth Edition, July 2007

ISBN 976-8142-07-3

Publisher's note:
This is a work of fiction. Names, characters, places and incidents are either the product of the authors' imagination or are used fictitiously, and any resemblance to actual persons, living or dead, events, or locales is entirely coincidental.

Contents

Foreword

This opportunity to introduce the first in a series of Belizean writers, many of whom I have the pleasure of knowing, provides me with an occasion to encourage the young or adult reader to soar to new heights through reading.

Much of our reading material presently comes from areas of the world with more developed societies with different values and exotic cultures. It is therefore particularly pleasurable for me to participate in promoting and supporting indigenous publishing. Efforts such as these will strengthen our own cultural values, broaden our vision, and increase our understanding of each other.

Reading has a vital role to play, not only as a tool of learning, but also as a pleasurable, recreational experience.

Living in the information age, our sensory perceptions are bombarded by the electronic media with pictures and sound bytes whether we desire it or not. But, no matter this bombardment reading is and will always be an essential skill and a route to adventure that constantly stimulates our imagination.

The motivation to read is an acquired skill and the start of an experience which will begin a journey into new knowledge, the higher realms of fantasy and imagination and the mystery of people's lives. Those who invest the time and energy necessary to become good readers derive great pleasure from reading.

Always read for pleasure; but also read for purpose. Read and think critically, always seeking to determine whether or not the writer's arguments are reasonable, balanced or totally off the wall. Read a variety of literature, not limiting yourself to the good romance novels or tabloids which we oftentimes enjoy. Investigate also the world of mystery novels, biographies... just allow reading and the pleasure of it to embrace you. In time, reading will become a good habit and a skill that will open a world of opportunities for you.

May the stories selected here bring the same pleasure to you as it did to me.

Joy Ysaguirre
Chief Librarian
Belize City, April 1995

Introduction

For several years now I have thought how valuable it would be to have a published anthology of the best of Belizean short fiction. Here now, under one cover, is some of Belize's best short fiction. We hope that the stories in this book will bring a great deal of enjoyment to those who journey through its pages.

Over the years a considerable body of literature has developed both about Belize and by Belizeans. The majority of texts about Belize have been written by visiting academics and scholars; unfortunately, most of these works are not well-known within the country itself. Likewise, works by Belizeans have not been widely available or known outside of Belize. This body of literature covers the spectrum from poetry to prose and has been written in English, Creole, and Spanish. The country has a particularly long tradition of journalism with numerous dailies and weeklies published during the past century. Currently one can choose from at least five or six newspapers each week. There have been other bits of literary production over the years but it has been during the past two decades that hundreds of articles, books, magazines, and collections have been published about or by Belizeans. Two major bibliographies, each containing hundreds of pages of references to works concerning Belize attest to the explosion in the production of Belizean texts. Professor Bruce Ergood goes so far as to call the period from 1980 to 1990 the 'golden age' of Belizean literature both because of the quantity and quality of production during that time. One cannot discuss Belizean literature without mentioning poetry and the novel. Several collections and anthologies of poetry have been published in Belize, many by the government print-ery. Several Belizeans have also written novels, the most important of which are *Beka Lamb* and *In Times Like These* both by Zee Edgell and both published internationally as a part of the Heinemann Caribbean Writers Series. This anthology does not cover poetry or novels but is only con-cerned with short fiction. Most of the stories included in this collection were first published either before or after Ergood's 'golden age' with the exception of the works of Zoila Ellis. In selecting the stories to be included in this collection, I limited myself to works that had been previ-ously published and that were written in either English or Creole. Thus I have not included any of the stories from *Old Benque* by David Ruiz Puga, a collection written in Spanish which represents a milestone in the history of Belizean literature because it is the first major literary text to be published only in Spanish in independent Belize.

This anthology has been prepared with the student in mind. First and foremost for the school children in Belize who will learn of their own literary heritage through its study. Secondly, this anthology should be a welcome addition to the collection of any student of Belize who is interested in the literary development and cultural identity of this coun-try. Many of these stories have not been available, except in the archives, for many years while others have only recent-ly been published in other collections by a single author.

The stories in this collection are as different and varied as are Belizeans themselves. The shortest piece in the collec-tion is 'Crab Seasin' from *A Child Remembers* by Evadne L. Wade-Garcia. Written entirely in Creole, it is a sweet remembrance of times gone by. This story was originally a part of a collection which won first prize in a writing competition held by the National Library Service in 1987.

There are two selections from *Pataki Full* by Colville Young, 'The Representative' and 'Sugar.' Young has been active in all aspects of Belizean cultural life for many years. He has written and published many plays but is perhaps best known for his collection of *Creole Proverbs* and his poetry. His two works in this anthology present the Belizean cynicism with politics as well as the effects of poverty on the dignity of rich and poor alike.

Zoila Ellis is represented in this anthology by the story 'The Teacher' from her book *On Heroes, Lizards and Passion*. Another of her stories, 'White Christmas an' Pink Jungle,' has also been anthologized in a collection of up and coming Caribbean authors entitled *Caribbean New Wave Anthology*.

'A Conscience for Christmas' has appeared in print twice before. Once as a part of Evan X Hyde's *Feelings* and once in a Christmas edition of the no-longer published magazine *Brukdown*. His story is a remarkable snapshot of Belizean life in the 1970's, yet the themes he explores are still current today.

Leo Bradley has two stories included in this anthology which are taken from two different collections published decades apart. Bradley was one of the first to become interested in collecting and preserving Belize's short fiction. Professor A.L. McLeod has called Bradley "without doubt the first identifiably Belizean writer of short fiction." 'Elastic Gold' from the collection *Among my Souvenirs* paints a vivid portrait of a Belizean fisherman in the period of World War II. 'The Day of the Bridge' is a contemporary story centered on one of the most familiar symbols of life in Belize City.

Like Bradley, Lawrence Vernon has distinguished himself in service to Belize as a librarian. 'The Third Wish' from the collection *Among my Souvenirs* is not an entirely original story – the same basic plot has been used by other authors. Vernon, however, makes the story distinctly Belizean and the ending is still a rather gruesome surprise to the unknowing.

John A. Watler was the third author whose works were included in *Among my Souvenirs*. His story from that collection included in this anthology makes use of an age-old plot device but is nonetheless an amusing read. 'Bitter-Sweet Revenge' makes for a somewhat lighter conclusion to what is otherwise a fairly serious collection of stories.

One of the great difficulties in assembling and editing such a collection has to do with the use of Belizean Creole. Since there is, as yet, no standard orthography, I have tried to be precise in spelling words exactly as the various authors have published them in the original.

The short fiction in this anthology represents work written over a period of some 40 years, years in which Belize has undergone enormous changes: Independence, the sugar boom, demographic shifts, the introduction of satellite television, the growth of tourism, and the emergence of gang violence to name but a few. This collection of short fiction presents small portraits, snapshots if you will, of the life and culture of this country. In its totality this anthology represents some of the finest writing ever published in Belize and together these individual snapshots make up an important page in the colourful photo album of Belizean life both past and present

Michael D. Phillips
Editor

astic Gold

 from *Among my Souvenirs*

by Leo Bradley

*L*ook, papa! There is a big piece! There! Look!"
The words were shouted with joyous flavour, and the cranky dorey almost overturned as the excited boy of fifteen pointed frantically at the crooked clump of mangrove bush trapping the dark bulk. The sharp but tired eyes of the aged fisherman turned with the agility that sprang from experience of the sea. They rested tensely on the bulk that lay in the path of the pointing fingers. And the ropy muscles of his hairy, salt-encrusted face palpitated. Sure enough it was rubber!

"Paddle fast, son. It is the stuff! It is rubber!"

Anxious strokes sent the tired dorey softly through the glossy green water, onto the mangrove shore. Quickly, anticipatingly, even before the dorey rammed its bow into the tendrils of the mangrove, the paddle of Max Flowers stretched out and prod the mass, and tested successfully its resilience. The rubber bulk trembled gently on the sandy bottom in two feet of water. Gosh! It was rubber, all right!

The excitement was heightened to fever pitch as not ten feet away, further among the crawling mangroves, hidden in debris of bits of weed and what not, was another mass, equally big, equally resilient.

"This is our day, Sonny! By Jove, this is our day!"

And the brawny arms of the tall fisherman, accustomed to haul in fish and raise sails, and fight weather, clasped the young shoulders of his son in the glee of satisfaction and realization.

Of course they then looked right and left along the crazy curves of the mangrove shore. But there were no more rubber bulks. But two was enough. And the experienced brain of Max Flowers, accustomed to assess quickly the weight of a big Jew Fish or the income accruing from a six-foot barracuda, worked quickly on the rubber. Yes, they were about two hundred pounds each in weight. At twenty cents a pound, that would fetch about eighty dollars. All this swam warmly in his mind as they secured the two masses of rubber and towed them to the little fishing boat balleting in the light swells near to the caye.

It was in early 1944, and the stretching coastline of Turneffe Caye lay bright and clear in the March sunrise, disappearing into little bits of land as it went its thirty-six miles down the emerald strip of sea that bordered it for a few yards off-shore. At the end of this green ribbon of water showed the brown and grey rocks of the reef almost in line with the intermittent sandy islets that ran down the coast. Then the blue, angry carpet of the Caribbean took over, spreading eastwards past the horizon. Its flowing swells shipped up by a strong south-easter wind ran rushing onto the islets and lost force gradually until they were mere ripples when they touched the mangrove roots of the mainland.

But out across the 'blue,' past Half Moon Caye and way out into the bolder breakers of the mid-Caribbean, German submarines were playing havoc at the time with American shipping that travelled from Latin America, bringing into their hatches the raw materials of war. How often had wrecked life-boats and floating bodies, and broken bits of spars and masts that found their way on the Belizean coast told the tale of midnight sinkings in the orgy of vicious warfare! And now the ships that bore the big bulks of rubber, perhaps coming direct from the virgin forests of the Amazon, vomited them unwillingly into the sea as torpedoes found their mark again and again. These masses of rubber floated among the flotsam and jetsam to lie finally among the mangroves of Turneffe Caye and several other islands. An agent in Belize City was paying twenty cents per pound for any bulk of rubber found and delivered. The recovered rubber was then sent to the United States for the great factories of war to make weapons to wage more war. Then it was that many a fisherman on the Belizean coast lay off the job of fishing and turned to this elastic gold that fetched such a price. There was scarcely any hardship involved. One only had to search and search among the mangroves, find the stuff, deliver it safely in Belize City, and collect a cheque. Why, some fishermen got rich within a week. Or nearly rich, bearing in mind their interpretation of the word.

Max Flowers was not among the fortunate ones. His fifty years told on him severely. Many a night, after combing the Turneffe coast, he sat in the bow of his boat after a supper of fried fish; and while Sonny slept after a hard day's hunting, he thought disappointedly of how elated he would be to find one bulk – just one bulk of rubber! But for four weeks now he had to return to Belize City after a relief catch of fish to cover expenses and leave some money home. And every time at the market wharf, sitting by the dancing fishing boats, he heard tales of great finds. Why, some fishermen found the bulks among the man-

groves just near to the city! And he would travel so far with
no bit of luck at this elastic gold. Even the tale of a strange
black boat from south chasing others and taking away the
bulks of rubber found no fear with him. If that boat caught
up with him, he would scarcely find a fish, much less a
bulk of rubber! But he would not give up. No, he wouldn't.
His little home by Racecourse Street needed strengthening.
Even fifty dollars would do the job. That must come from
rubber. He must try again and again.

And now, as the little craft lay quietly behind the tiny
caye, and the flooding moonlight poured its silver beams
snakily along the transparent water, Max Flowers passed
his hand satisfyingly along the cruffy surface of the rubber
bulks safely stowed in the boat. Sonny lay sleeping. But
Max could not sleep The cool breeze that raised the roar of
the surf by the reef and sang melodies in the nearby coconut trees also played on his weather-beaten face that was
not cringed with worries tonight, but calm with satisfaction
eighty dollars. Imagine, eighty dollars earned in ten minutes. Now the house could be strengthened and Sonny
could start his savings bank account. No, none of the many
nights when he had had his boat heavy with bony fish or
snapper could measure up to the exhilaration of this night.
And when his light thoughts tapered off into sleep, it was
one of no dreams, no worries, just a long night-time of
sweet nothingness.

The pale silver of the retreating moonlight gave way to
the pursuing purple clouds scratching the sky in the East,
and the faint light which ushered in the royal pageantry of
tropic sunrise. Molten yellow sprinkled right and left and
above in long rays as the great ball of gold appeared regal-
ly in a chariot of multi-coloured clouds, and threw its glory
far afield. It brightened the dull green of the mangroves

and accentuated the motion of the sea. It danced amidst the coconut branches and threw soft shadows by the yellow crabs basking on the white beach. It generated new energy in Max Flowers as he stretched and awoke to the life of a new day. No, no fishing for him and Sonny today. It was Belize City right away – right after a quick breakfast.

The little craft crept slowly out to sea and accelerated its path through the waves as the puffs of wind filled the belly of its sail. Round the mangrove points it went – through the broad lagoon of Turneffe – further and further west towards Belize City and eighty dollars.

It was Sonny who saw it, and watched it follow continuously.

"Papa."

"Yes, son."

"There is a black boat following us."

Max turned sidewards a little faster than usual. Sure enough, just edging the mangrove shore, a black boat about twice the length of his was just beginning to lay its course straight for them.

"Where did it come from! Did you see!"

"It was anchored by that patch of bush to the South, dad. Then a little time ago it hoisted sail. Papa could it be...?"

"Shut up, son, I don't know!"

But if he didn't know, he certainly suspected what was also running through Sonny's mind. When he looked again it seemed as if the black craft dipping in the waves had gained half of the mile which had separated them. It was coming with a dead fair wind – and directly at them too!

"No," thought Max Flowers; "no crook will take away these pieces of rubber. No, it's not fair. If I have to die they will not have them!"

And now his great experience of sailing welled up at

this hour of suspense. Give the boat full sail. Throw overboard the two bags of sand I was taking to fill our yard. Sonny, haul in the jib more closely. Sit over that side so as not to slow up the boat. By Jove, they won't catch us – not today!

And with that firm determination the little craft seemed to answer royally. It struggled atop the oncoming waves, darting forward with renewed force. Sonny Flowers held eyes glued on the black vessel. Now he could see two men in it. She was not gaining any longer. But not being left behind either. But Max Flowers had no inclination to look backward. His mind and heart and eye were on his boat, begging every bit of wind in his sail and jib, maneuvering the helm to gain distance by every trick of mathematics and navigation.

Soon the two boats sailed slowly through the quiet Grand Bogue Creek, some distance apart, and then out of the western mangroves of Turneffe. The green shore water once more turned to blue with the long, lingering swells. And now Max pointed the bow of his obedient craft straight for Sergeant's Caye, which lifted its leafy head above the twelve miles of sea in a straight line with English and Goff's Cayes.

And on and on came the black boat, like something sinister and sinful. For once Max Flowers wondered, however, if it was really chasing them for rubber. Perhaps someone was sick aboard her. Yet she would not have come so far – so persistently.

The mid-day sun was now high overhead, colouring the water a brilliant blue that burned the eyes. At its bow the craft felt the repeated bursts of spray that sprang saltly into the eyes of Max and his son. At times it seemed the boat was going under water, but Max Flowers held it at bay, not retreating one inch from his feverish bid for every bit of agility in it. And the wind answered to his determination. It gave him the same power that filled the sail of the black boat. Only he added his experience of sail-craft, and if he could not get away, at least the pursuer could not get closer either.

Soon they passed through the channel by Sergeant's Caye, and at the same distance back the black craft came through also.

"Papa, why do they keep coming? They are not gaining."

"They hope to catch us near to the Bogue, son. The currents are tricky there."

The stretch of low-lying islands some seven miles from Belize City had several openings or little channels through which the fish-boats passed. The currents, complicated by the normal channel currents, plus the swells coming from across the 'blue' plus the reaction of the far flow-out of the Belize River all combined to speed or slow the sailing of a boat. The mariners of the black boat probably knew all this, and knew the correct opening to take. If they did so, they could easily catch up on Max Flowers.

But Max Flowers knew all this too. He was not taking the normal openings. He pointed the bow of his boat towards the southern point of Water Caye which stretched by the Bogue. The black craft could not alter to this direction, as its sailors were already heading for the opening they judged the best. It appeared as if Max would take the long way around.

"Daddy, they will catch up on us this way. Daddy, are you sure you know what you are doing?"

"Take it easy, son, this time I shall fool them."

Neither of the two spoke, and Max still worked at

straining every bit of expertise from his little craft. Now and then he touched the big bales of rubber for courage.

Then when he was just by the narrow opening of a little channel towards the direction he was going, he suddenly altered course, and sailed quickly through this opening. At that time the black boat was also sailing through an opening further north. But this was the trick. For when Max sailed his little craft through on the other side and could see Belize City several miles away, he was now in a position where he got the full force of a fair wind, while the black boat had to sail on a quarter.

Now with this big advantage the little craft slowly but consistently left the black boat behind. Sonny could not believe his eyes. He could only watch up at his dad silently, while he had a smile of conquest on his lips. And as the buildings of Belize City got bigger over the waters, so did the black craft get smaller behind them, until all of a sudden, the black boat altered course and turned back, most likely to lay await for some other fisherman.

It was two o'clock when the boat entered the estuary of the Belize River and tied up by the customs wharf. The red-topped building and blazing crimson bouganvilleas by the Fort seemed to join in the joy of the two victors. Wet and tired, they bore the heavy bulks to the warehouse. And when they returned to their craft to sail her across the river to its Yarborough mooring, it was not with speed nor anxiety. It was with the cool feeling of a job well accomplished. A green cheque marked eighty dollars reposed comfortably in the tattered but firmly-buttoned pocket of the fisherman's shirt.

epresentative

 from *Pataki Full*

by Colville Young

*I*t was mid-May. From early January that year it had not rained a drop.

Families that depended on vats for their water supply had taken to locking their faucets at night; begging, stealing or (as a last resort) buying a bucket of water had become increasingly common. Many who had never used the city's water system because, having vats, they regarded it as an unnecessary expense, had grudgingly paid WASA and had the vital connection made.

Then, a week ago, the rains had come. Intermittently, for one solid week shower after shower had pounded Belize City with tropical intensity. The browning grass had already begun to look green and threatened to grow waist-high almost overnight.

Wishwilly Street, from being a dry dirt-road where the wind daily swept swirls of dust into the homes that bordered it, became a stagnant stream whose waters extended into the unfenced yards of the neighbourhood.

For a day, the rains had stopped. The angry grey clouds had disappeared and the sun shone savagely on the flooded world beneath. Most of the water had already run off the

27

street. (One of the mysterious things about Belize City is that, although most of it is only a foot or so above sea-level – some say below – and in spite of its primitive drainage system, flooded streets are generally back to normal, given a twenty-four hour let up in the downpour).

Of course, water remained in the innumerable potholes in the street. As to the yards, most of them were totally covered. In these unwanted backyard pools swam mosquito larvae and tadpoles and the overnight spawnings of the finger-long fish locally called poopsies. At night armies of newly metamorphosed frogs lifted their voices in loud, mournful chorus.

The Honourable Jonas Harold Parker ('the silver tongued talker') was, unusually, visiting his constituency. It is true that the next election was not due till the end of the year, but the party leader had given him an ultimatum. He had neglected his area for four years. Then in this fifth year he had allowed the dry season to pass idly by. So today, in spite of the water-filled potholes, he had parked his air-conditioned Buick on the edge of his division and was canvassing house to house. He wore his friendliest smile, had his warmest hugs ready for the ladies, and his most confidence-inspiring handshakes available for the men. He had also decided to take a few of the children into his arms in spite of the accident that had literally messed up an expensive shirt the last time he had gone visiting. God, what a smell it had been! What did they feed those kids on anyway, he wondered.

He paused cautiously before the first house on Wishwilly Street. He tried to remember who lived in this shanty. Flowers? Smith? Jones? Williams? After four years it was all as vague as outlines of trees in a fog. He fished a street list out of his briefcase and consulted it expertly. Jones! That was it, of course.

He looked skeptically at the lengths of wood set on blocks which formed a precarious bridge over the water from the street side to the house's doorway. He sighed and for the thousandth time wondered why he did not take his wife's advice and leave politics; but he knew very well what the reasons were: the three p's, as he wittily put it in private converse with his fellow assemblymen – power, paycheck and (whisper it) the undoubted perks. These perks were certainly immoral, probably quite often illegal; but, then, how was a fellow to support a wife and two children on less than four thousand a month?

Carefully keeping his balance, he safely negotiated the rickety bridge and knocked at the door. A girl of about eight peeped out. Her hair was plaited in corn-rows, and she was very dark.

"What you want?" she asked ungraciously, staring at him from head to toe with undisguised hostility. Even though he had put on his oldest and (relatively speaking) shabbiest clothes, he was too well-dressed.

"Is Miss Jones at home?" he asked, expertly searching his pockets for a candy.

"Nobody live here name so," replied the child, getting ready to close the door.

"Isn't your mother in?" the visitor tried again, slipping the sweet to the girl.

"Only me an me bredda at home," was the reply, not yet in a welcoming voice but a little warmer following a greedy clutch at the bribe.

The door had been opened a few more inches, enabling the Honourable Parker to see into the room.

"Who you, sah?" asked the girl. At last native inquisitiveness had taken over and the campaigner, seasoned as he was, quickly seized the initiative.

"Haven't you heard the name of your representative, the honourable Jonas Parker? No? I wonder what they teach in schools these days! Anyway, little girl, it's due to me and my government that there is prosperity in this land. Without me there would not be that street for you to walk on."

He paused to point shamelessly at the cratered stretch of mud outside.

"And it is because of me that when Christmas comes there is turkey and ham on your table. And it is because of me that you have the TV set and that beautiful stereo over there in the corner."

The little girl's eyes grew rounder and rounder with dawning comprehension.

"Then you da no no Parker or Farker or Sharker! Why you never tell de struth fram de start? Barney! Look who come! Uncle Bill come visit we from Los Angeles!"

A strapping youth of fifteen or sixteen came to the door.

"Good morning Mr. Jones," said the honourable visitor. "I hope you will be good enough to allow me to come in, have a seat and talk a little."

"Talk 'bout what?" growled the newcomer. "Me no name Jones; and as to you, you da no we Uncle Bill. Who de hell you, and what you doin' in dis part of town? Lost you way, or what?"

"So the Jones family don't live here any more. I see! Anyway, what I have to say concern you just as much though you don't look like you could get on the register of voters in time for December. How old are you, my good man?"

"Just as you say, too young to vote. And even if I was ole 'nuff, too wise to vote for a rip-off artist like you."

"Look here, you young loafer, have some respect! Do

you realize who you're addressing? If this is the kind of attitude you're growing up with you will always be stuck in this swamp. Why don't you go out and get a job, eh? Why don't you learn a trade, eh? What do you expect to do, go through life sorry for yourself and vexed with the world of those who are successful?"

Suddenly, he realized that he had been too impulsive, had taken the wrong tone. After all, even if these kids couldn't vote, their mother could. As effortlessly as changing gears he removed the anger from his deep resonant voice.

"Of course, son, you are not really to blame for your poverty. 1 know it's a burden, just as the responsibility of representing the ambitious people of this neighbourhood is a burden for me. But we must neither of us despair, we must neither of us give up the struggle to achieve a better life for this beautiful jewel of our glorious Mayan ancestors. Now, I know times are hard, I know what the cost of living is like, I know how unfair it seems that you barely have enough to keep body and soul together while others can bathe in Johnny Walker Black if they want to. But that's exactly why you need a champion like Jonas Parker, the worker's friend, in the National Assembly. So tell your mammy I'll be back when she's at home, and will talk to her. Meanwhile, to help you stay out of trouble, here's a little present."

He shook hands with the young man, at the same time pressing a five dollar bill into the reluctant palm he was grasping. A moment later he was balancing his way back over the wobbly bridge.

Safely on the street again, he breathed a loud sigh. If that encounter was any barometer, this year's campaign promised to be an uphill struggle, a very uphill struggle.

By tomorrow the first mosquitoes of the rainy season would be out. A day or two after that they would by hungrily swarming everywhere in this part of the city. He was touched with an uneasy sense of wonder at the survival of 'these people' as he called them in his mind.

Framed by the doorway of the house he had just left, the young man and his sister stood holding hands, his left in her right. With his other hand he rustled the bill in his pocket as if to make certain it was still there. The girl sucked fiercely at her sweet. They both watched him go with enigmatic brown eyes and totally expressionless faces.

"Mary livin' well while Marta ketching hell," said the young man grimly. He gently drew his sister into the room and closed the door.

They would be growing up soon.

nscience
or Christmas

 Feelings

 Evan X Hyde

*S*o, it was Christmas Eve. After five now, and the foggy dusk beginning to lie down on top of Belize City. The office Christmas party had started, but it seemed to him everybody was trying to get too happy too quickly. You worked for a whole year in an office and hated it, and because it's Christmas and the boss make a lot of money, suddenly you're supposed to eat, drink, dance, and be merry. Bull shit, he was going home to smoke and rest; later in the night he would bathe and put on some clean threads and go back to the party. By then, many of them would be stoned to the bone, and if he saw anybody suitable, he would move her off and take her somewhere where they could be together.

There were people on the streets, but he wasn't looking to see any of them. He didn't care. He was alone, and that was the way he mostly remembered it, and in fact that was the way he liked it. There was money in his pocket. He was a checking clerk in the warehouse, and he hustled, not big so the boss could notice it, but steadily and profitably. He didn't see anything wrong with it. Everybody was doing it. Christmas was always the best time to hustle; then there

37

was his Christmas bonus in his pocket. With money, you were something; without it, you were nothing.

He was in the Lake now, homegrounds. Adeste Fideles, a big box, was blasting O come, all ye faithful business. To where and for what? Faithful to whom for what and how long? They never bothered to explain themselves. Children were chasing each other in the street ahead of him, their skin showing through their tattered clothes. Santa was on his way, filled his sleigh with good things, but only for a precious few. These cowboys, indians, and sheriffs back here in the Lake wouldn't see too many good things. But what difference did it make? He couldn't change it. He remembered his great aunt before she died saying to him, "Look out for yourself, boy, look out for yourself."

He was home now, three rooms, a small kitchen, dining room, and a big bedroom. He turned on the lights. There were new curtains and linoleum. His sister had done everything. He took a stout from the refridge, sat down by a window in the dining room. Drinking it, he caught the neighbour peeking at him through her blinds. Old women were like that, obsessed by young, single men, their comings and goings and their doings. It would be too bad if his sister became like that, but maybe it was inevitable. She had always been like a mother to him.

It was after six. He went into the bedroom and turned on the radio; they were talking about Navidad. He turned it off and put a King Cole Christmas record on his record player. 'Little Christmas Tree': his favourite Christmas song.

He stripped to his underclothes, and lay in bed with Mr. Cole still singing. He wanted to smoke, but decided he would save the cream till later. There was no Christmas tree in the house. His son was in the States along with his mother. He wouldn't know him. It was easier that way, he guessed

When he awoke, he figured it was after midnight, but the transistor said minutes to ten. Damn, he'd left the lights and record player on. Burning money. They were broadcasting messages from people overseas. Christmas was a sentimental time.

His clothes were already pressed. Blue was his speed tonight. A girl in the States had sent him a blue Superfly hat and a blue silk shirt with blue velvet at the collar and end of the long sleeves. Dan arranged the pants, smooth blue polyester with bells at the bottom to hang over black high heeled boots. Moving through a store, he had found a blue silk handkerchief to put everything together.

He bathed downstairs and it was chilly. In the bedroom, he shaved with a two track Gillette razor, using warm water from an 'icy hot' and Old Spice shaving cream. He splashed Yardley's after shave on his face, then some white Johnson's baby powder to take off the shine. Brut deodorant and Brut cologne next, sprinkling the cologne into the blue silk handkerchief. Most of these expensive preparations were from ships. He had friends on the waterfront. Taking off his robe, he put on clean underclothes, then the blue shirt and pants, and a black boots. Afro sheen for his hair, a pick, the blue Superfly hat, and now he was ready, except for a smooth.

He put on Jimmy Smith, rolled a smoke, and got another stout. When he sat by the dining room window, smoking along with Mr. Smith, the old woman was there watching.

When he left home, he was feeling clean and mellow. Going to town, he saw many people coming back now with big parcels. Santa was working overtime. A drunk he knew by sight lay partly in the drain. This fellow's Christmas had ended before it started. The women he passed looked so clean and smelled so beautiful he smiled in private satisfaction. Before morning, he would have one of these women in his arms and he would be explaining how much he loved her and needed her and she would tremble and moan and they would go home for Christmas.

As he turned the corner of Vernon Street into Magazine Road, he couldn't believe his eyes. It looked like a fellow was mugging an old woman, trying to tear away her purse. He shouted and broke into a run, the high heels clumsy on his feet. The mugger sprinted away into the opposite direction, right into the headlights of a police jeep turning from Cemetery into Magazine. Paramilitary were jumping out of the screeching jeep as the mugger froze in fright and they grabbed him roughly and bent his hand behind his back.

He stood now and watched as the group of them triumphantly brought the mugger. Geez, it was only a boy, his eyes painful from the hand they appeared about to break. A child attacking an old woman for money. He felt a little sick, the lights from the jeep still glaring in his eyes, as the corporal in charge questioned him, and he walked back to the old woman followed by the paramilitary, because he did not feel like talking. She did not appear to be hurt and really looked like a sprightly old type. The boy mugger had picked on an old brammer for a victim, throwing culo when he thought he was throwing luck. But she refused to press charges, saying the child was only a boy, and he followed her cue, telling the corporal he had not seen anything really. The corporal and paramilitary did not seem eager to release the boy. It looked like there was blood in their eyes, but there were two witnesses, so after some hard words to the boy and some more hand bending they shoved him down the street.

The woman and he were still standing there as the jeep moved on. He felt somewhat awkward, but she said: "I know you. You are Caldo, the son of John and Mary. I am Miss Gertrude. I thank you for your help and I want you to come to my house for a drink of wine before you go on your way. He hesitated. "Please," she said, and he went along with her, wondering how this was happening to him on a night like this. Christmas Eve was one night you did not spend with old women, and yet as she spoke to him, he admired her, the life, youth, and spunks within her. He smiled quietly as she told him not to think that she was courting him.

Caldo thought to himself as the old woman rattled on, that Miss Gertrude was lonely, she wanted someone to talk to. But he regretted thinking it as he did so. It was cheap of him to judge her like that, to assume she was using him to escape her loneliness.

"Here we are. It is I alone at home," laughed Miss Gertrude. "My granddaughter has gone to a party. She is too young, but it is with a friend, so I sent her. Nobody goes to church any more."

He could see and smell Christmas in here. Black cake and ham, turkey, the crisp store smell of new linoleum and curtains and varnish and paint. A brightly decorated Christmas tree with angel hair blinking with colourful lights and presents underneath. This was a home at Christmas when he was a boy.

"Christmas is for the children," she said, interrupting his thoughts. "That boy tonight was just a child. It is bad there is no one to make his Christmas merry. My granddaughter Tricia she is only a child too, but she wants to be a woman."

She brought the wine in a bottle and a glass with two cubes of ice. He poured the wine on the ice and left it to chill.

"You are a child. O it is true, with women you are a great man, but to God you are just a sweet little baby boy."

He smiled again, wryly, but said nothing.

"Are you going to church tonight?"

"No. To a little party."

"I knew you were not going to church. The way you are dressed you are out to charm the ladies. You like many ladies, and you think you are a hero, but you are only running away from yourself."

The wine was very good, traditional Belize berry wine.

"Your wine is very good. It reminds me of wine my grandaunt used to give me at Christmas."

"Yes, it is from 1947. The older, the better."

"Like you," he said.

"Yes, I am 72 and I still wash and cook and scrub."

"You look very good for your age."

"I treat others the way I want them to treat me. I believe in God. Do you?"

"Yes, sometimes. I must go now. Thank you for the wine."

"Thank you for your help, young man, and try to believe all the time." He realized she wanted to speak some more, but she did not try to detain him.

Outside, the night wind was cool on his face. Inside Miss Gertrude's home had been warm and cosy, but time was moving past him now. Damn, almost twelve, party must be over by now.

But it wasn't over, just that it wasn't an office Christmas party any more. It was a Christmas party period; there were some strange faces in there, more women than men, and that was all right.

Before he reached the bar Joanna, the office receptionist had her hands on him and was telling him how beautiful he looked. But Caldo had no time for Joanna, never did, especially now she was high. Joanna, moreover, was pregnant, and looking for a daddy. You had to be smart to see it, and Caldo was smart. Shaking off Joanna, he noticed a woman in a soft yellow dress looking at him, but right then he wanted a stout.

The boys at the bar were mostly drunk, and it was all he could do to keep them from clawing on him and spitting stale alcohol in his face. People who were drunk mostly made him uncomfortable; one time he even had to pay money at court for punching a drunk at a dance who clawed in between Caldo and his partner. Good people made fools of themselves when they were drunk. Look at Joe, married man who didn't drink much usually, all messed up drunk and trying to dance with a sexy woman. She was leading the fool on. Some of the boys started urging Joanna to do a strip tease. She looked wild enough to do it.

Holding his stout carefully, he moved closer to the orchestra and almost tripped over a lady in soft yellow. As he stepped back to apologize, she smiled don't mention it and he could see that she was younger than she had appeared at first glance. It was hard to tell. Maybe she was old enough to be a woman, just that she had not suffered all the frustrations and pains which put lines in a woman's face, anxiety in her eyes, and desperation in her mind.

Damn, but she was fine like wine. Her eyes were soft pools of innocence and invitation, her cheeks were full, and her lips wet. You looked at her in the soft yellow maxi and you could see there was somebody in there to hold on to.

He looked in her eyes again and she said: "I came with Joanna." That was bad, very bad, he thought to himself. Joanna used younger girls to hustle men with. She took them to dances to bait the older men into spending their money hoping for a taste of the cream. Joanna changed girls every now and then, for sometimes, inevitably, the girls would meet a dude who'd blow their minds and they would run from Joanna's clutches.

He did not judge Joanna; she was a hustler, on the downhill side now, using her experience to stay in play, to be wherever the action was at, Island, or Rivers or Harbour Lights. And if Joanna had her way, soon this excitement in yellow would be just like her, hustling beers and beans and men wherever the lights were low, music was playing, and money was spending.

Caldo did not throw stones, for he was not without sin. Life, to him, it was for the strong. The strong used the weak to feed their strength. He was a man who needed women; he chose those he considered available and used them to satisfy his lust for excitement. There was not much emotion involved any more, just excitement. Love was a game people played, each trying to excite the other into panic. When you panicked, you lost, and Caldo did not panic any more, not even inside. He was cool and smooth and looking at this girl in yellow on Christmas Eve he knew what he would do and how he would do it. His Christmas would be soft yellow.

"Your glass is empty. Would you like something?"

"Yes, please. Whisky with water." She laughed slightly, betraying her inexperience. Whisky she was till experimenting with. It was not yet an acquired taste. Where this child get all these manners from, yes please, he hadn't heard that in a long time. She was genuine, that was what she was, genuine, was it because she was drinking? A sympathetic feeling ran inside him suddenly and he shook it off. When one was working, one could not be sympathetic.

What was the matter with him? If he didn't do it, some-body else would, and where would he be? On the outside looking in with a handful of regrets.

He put enough water in her whisky to soften the taste a little. The boys at the bar were still spitting stale alcohol. Freddie was asleep in a chair, and Christmas Eve lover boy Joe was slobbering in sexy woman's ear.

The band started 'Little Christmas Tree.' No one to buy you, give yourself to me. He set the drink beside her on a table and when she reached for it he held her hand and said no, let's dance. When she got up, he could see her backside was high and bouncy. She came into his arms without fear and her eyes were sparkling and dancing. He held her close; she danced slowly with him. She was on her toes and her head was on his shoulders. She smelled of nice perfume and powder. He knew her eyes were closed and he could feel her breasts against his chest, and he felt desire stirring in him.

When the piece finished, she stood quietly. Joe and Joanna were watching them, Joe from near the bar, Joanna from near the door. As the next piece started and he held her close, Caldo knew he would soon leave. Dancing he saw it as a ritual you engaged in before you had sex. While dancing, you decided if you were compatible. If you were compatible, you went somewhere; if you were not, you stopped dancing and looked for somebody else. He did not understand how some people could dance together for hours and not want to go home. Maybe he was different. So what? He was just different, and that was that. Joe was coming their way. Old office worker, married to a good woman, with some good children, yet he was always jeal-ous of Caldo, always throwing remarks about Caldo and the girls he heard Caldo was with. He was coming now to interfere. Why a married man, a family man, always feel like a single man having all the fun? Why a one woman man worry so much about a man on the move? Many times a man fool around with a lot of women because he is searching for the one who can make him settle down. Guys like Joe who already found a good woman should thank the Lord above for a faithful wife instead of envying the Lone Ranger. The grass, Caldo figured, must look greener from the other side of the fence. Joe, he said in his mind, don't come here messing with me and this girl. Not this time, Joe. But Joe had his hand on Caldo's shoulder now, and he turned around and pushed him hard and he fell down and started to vomit on the floor, like a dog, Caldo thought.

"Get your bag. Let's go."

"But I have to tell Joanna."

"Joanna, shit," he said.

And as they walked towards to door, Joanna's drunken, bitchy voice screamed in his ears. "And where do you two think you're going, Mr. Caldo?" He slapped Joanna. The band had stopped playing as he walked out with the girl in the yellow maxi. What was the matter with him? He wasn't drunk. He was just tired of being smooth with fools.

He asked her how old she was and she said eighteen and what was her name and she said Tricia and he remembered something but exactly what it was escaped him.

"Where are we going?" she asked.

"Home."

"Did you ask me?"

"No," he said. "I love you."

She held his arm and looked up at him. Her eyes were wet. "Do you mean it, Caldo? Please say you mean it, Caldo. I love you from a long time. I see you going to work, sometimes at nights I watch you passing with girls. I want to be with you. Caldo, anywhere you go, please." She was crying softly on his chest.

He felt a complete fool. He wanted to tell her to stop crying on his shirt or she would mess it up. But Caldo knew this was one girl he could never do that to. She was a child at heart, and Christmas, he mused to himself, it was for children. Run away, Caldo, he said to himself, run away from her, or she will be the end of you. Run away now, Caldo, run away from the softness of your heart.

He remembered her now. She was a primary school teacher. He'd seen her in uniform before, but never in a soft yellow maxi. No, Caldo, take her home with you. She will be so easy. When you are finished, wash your hands, wipe your mouth, and move on, move on.

He kissed her quickly to gain time. She wanted to linger, but he would not.

"Let's go," he held her hand. "What are you doing hanging around with Joanna? Don't you know what she is?" His voice was gruff.

"I wanted to go to the party. I knew you would be there. My grandmother didn't want to send me. Are you vex?"

"Who's your grandmother?"

"Miss Gertrude, don't –?"

He couldn't hear any more. Damn, there was a jinx on him. This was obeah business. Miss Gertrude, the little old woman who melted his heart on Christmas Eve. And now it was Christmas and her granddaughter was eating out what was left of his heart. Him, Caldo, Caldo the executioner, Lone Ranger Caldo, smooth Caldo, he was caught, trapped.

Damn, come on, girl, let's go home by Miss Gertrude. We'll drink the berry wine, the three of us, we'll talk, laugh and be merry. When the cock crows, we'll go to church, the three of us, what a way, and then we'll walk the streets and watch the children playing, the drunks and serenaders, me and you and Miss Granny. We'll visit my sister and your people. Damn, I'll take you and Miss Gertrude to my home. Christmas comes but once a year. He looked down at her. She was just a baby girl, and Christmas was for children.

4

The

eacher

from On Heroes, Lizards
and Passion

 Zoila Ellis

*T*eacher never forgot the day old Ramsey died. He arose as usual, at five a.m., said his morning prayers and after dousing his face in the washbasin by the chest of drawers, he picked up the slop bucket and proceeded outside. The morning was a faint purple colour rapidly fading to beautiful hues of pale violet and shell pink as the mist cleared and daybreak came.

He pulled the opening of his pale blue flannel pyjama shirt together as the cold air teased goose pimples on his chest and he made his way briskly down the stony path to the latrine. As he walked, he heard a cock crow in the distance, and then an answering crow from Miss Mangar's yard. "Miss Mangar rooster noisy jus' like she," he thought to himself. Every morning that he heard the rooster crow he thought the same thing, but he would never tell Miss Mangar that to her face. She was his good neighbour and had been his good friend ever since he had come down to teach at Cucumber Bank three years before.

When he finished emptying the bucket he left it there and walked back up to his house. Stooping by his doorway he pulled some fevergrass tea from a large bush and took it inside the house, scraping his boots on the step before entering. He went by his two-hole kerosene stove and lit it. Then he put on a skillet half-full of water to boil.

He stood by the doorway with a cup of water in one hand his toothbrush in the other. He filled his mouth with water from the cup, threw, back his head, gargled noisily and spat as far as he could. He did this three or four times enjoying the feel of cool water in his throat. Then he began brushing his teeth. From where he stood he could see the sun slowly rising up in waves of soft orange light from behind the hills. Every morning he brushed his teeth around this time so he could savour this sight. As he waited almost breathlessly for the first tip of gold to show itself, he felt an almost child-like joy. It was always the same lift of spirit that he experienced. Everytime. "The Lord is my Shepherd, I shall not want" he whispered to himself, feeling at peace with the world.

Humming, he dropped the bundle of fevergrass tea into the skillet and was soon – sniffing the fragrant aroma of lemon that wafted through the house. He sliced some of the creole bread that Miss Mangar had sent him the day before and, as he munched slowly through its delicious softness, he thought about all the things he had to do that day. Standard Six was preparing a play for the end of year entertainment, and he had to help them with that. The Education Officer was coming to supervise Miss Logan's teaching practice so he had to prepare her for that and plan a staff meeting for Friday. It was surprising how a Principal for such a small school of one hundred souls, had so much to do. Still, it kept him busy and he was happy. In this little community of Cucumber Bank he had found some peace. It was precious.

Not knowing where his thoughts might stray and wanting to avoid all sombreness, he leapt up and completed his dressing for school. He picked up the only two books he had in his bookcase – a teacher's manual and Students Companion – and set out.

The sun was pale yellow on the crest of the distant hills, giving no warmth. Teacher took his usual route to school, walking slowly along the worn path edged with long razor-grass which was still wet with dew. In some parts the dirt was soft, almost mud, and he had to slow down even more so that he would not slip. The path edged the riverbank in many parts and as he walked Teacher looked down on the Old Belize River, broodingly calm under a sheet of thin mist. Broad and lazy, it snaked down for miles with the same deceptive gentleness giving the unwary no hint of its power, or of its secrets. Sometimes it stayed asleep all year, burying itself close to the earth until the villagers thought the river would disappear. Teacher remembered the first month he had been here when it seemed the river would go to sleep forever under the blazing July sun. Then suddenly the rains had come. For days and nights it rained, lashing the earth with stinging blows, unleashing thunder and light-ning and screaming winds. The farmers had called it a freak storm, and when it was over, the river awoke. It rose swiftly, surely, implacably from its bed and stretched itself, covering almost the entire land around it with water. Houses were washed away. Cattle, pigs and chickens drowned. Miss Mangar's little boy had died. He himself had lost his books, a loss he still mourned. He had trea-sured those books. They had lived with him. In the time of his anguish they had watched him and he had felt that they understood. Then the river had taken them and he had wept, hating the river...

"Now I have learnt to respect this river," he thought to himself as he walked. "It is strong yet gentle. It has power yet does not abuse it. Perhaps at the time of the storm it was angry that someone like me had come to drink from its waters." He smiled at his own fancifulness.

Soon he reached the bend in the path which took him away from the riverbank and he stopped to wipe the mud off his shoes. It was quiet except for the sound of someone chopping wood. He figured it would be Mr. Mangar. He would stop and remind him about the Parent/Teachers meeting this evening. He saw Mr. Mangar by the big breadfruit tree. His gnarled black hands gripped a sturdy axe hoisted high above his greying head. Teacher watched as it came crashing down steadily on a thick piece of wood. Mr. Mangar must have seen him coming for he slowly lowered the axe and turned to him, wiping the sweat off his face with the back of his hand.

"Morning Teecha. Bella!" he shouted toward the house.

"Yes Mista Harry?" A woman inside hollered back.

"Teecha di pass. Gi ah di news no gyal?"

Mr. Mangar waited as his wife, a stout brown-skinned woman with long black hair, came to the door and then ran down the short path to meet Teacher. Teacher never failed to marvel to himself at how nimble she was for her size. She was twice as big as Mr. Mangar yet she moved twice as fast. However, she called her gentleman, like the rest of the community, "Mista Harry."

"Mornin' Teecha. How di mawnin'?"

"Good morning, Miss Bella. I'm fine, thank you. That creole bread was very delicious."

"Oh! Dat's notting. How di rheumatism, Teecha? Yu did drink da bush ah did give yu fi boil?"

"Yes I did, but I am determined to let nature take its course and I guess I will just have to learn to live with it."

"Da true dat. Teecha yu yer sey Mista Ramsey deh 'pon dying?"

"Really?"

"Me jus' yer it dis mawnin'. Miss Maisie son pass gawn up ribba an he stop fi sey i ma sen fi tell mi. Poor Miss Maisie!"

"But weren't they expecting it?"

"Yes! Yes! But still you know, when you expec' someting fi happen and when it happen fi true da two diffrant someting."

Later, continuing on his way to school, he reflected on Miss Bella's understanding and her calm view of life. He remembered when her only son had died, washed away by the flood that time. She never found him. Neighbours had been afraid she would break down, she had remained so quiet and numb. They had sent for Teacher to talk to her, and he had come, hardly knowing any of them, still hurt over the loss of his beloved books. He had seen her that evening sitting alone in the darkening parlour and staring out the window at the brown water still high on the bank. All around had been the raw smell of the mud the river had left behind. He had gone up to her and quietly taken her hand in his. Gently he had held it as one holds a newborn bird. "Do you want to pray?" He had asked her softly. She had made no sign that she had heard him.

For a long time he had just sat with her on the couch by the window holding her hand, saying nothing, searching for the right words, the right actions. Then he had begun to talk to her hoping that somehow his sympathy and his feelings would flow out of his fingers and unlock her grief.

"I too feel the grief frozen in me. I too watch the river, hating it, for it has taken away from me the last thing dear and precious to me. But it seems that I cannot weep anymore although, like you, I should. I ask you if you want to pray but for a long time now I have been without prayers, without belief in God and good. When I wanted it again it was gone, gone, gone."

He had not felt himself grip her hand painfully but he must have had, for she had cried out. As if that cry had triggered a need, she had begun to tremble like a leaf in a hurricane, shaking uncontrollably in deep spasms of grief.

She had wept for a long time into the darkening night and Teacher had held her.

In the morning, as he had packed his things before he left, she had said sadly:

"Tenk yu Teecha. I alright now. Da so life go."

Thereafter, he had looked back on that incident as the beginning of his rebirth.

As he walked the last few minutes to school he remembered St. Jude's Mission without the usual pain.

Why had he become a priest? He couldn't remember except that his mother had been so happy and proud of him.

The good Catholic Fathers had sent him to high school and she had been grateful. Wanting to return the favour she had convinced him. Had he ever felt happy as a priest? He couldn't remember.

The time of his entering the priesthood had been right. The mood of the country had been violently anti-British and Nationalistic sentiments were aroused. It was the fifties. A native priest had seemed an excellent idea. He had been an excellent idea – loyal, black, grateful.

His rebelliousness had been a shock to his superior. Or rather, the Bishop had called it rebelliousness. He himself would never have called it that. Not at first.

"In the beginning I was happy," he thought. "The first year of my priesthood, when they sent me to the remote Kekchi Indian village to teach. I tried to teach the people about the way to organise and get better prices for their corn. That's all." The Bishops had soon sent for him, on the grounds that they had reports of his subversive activities. Maybe that was when they had begun to watch him. Or was it later – when he had started the youth group? Anyway, whatever it was, he had been recalled, scolded, and then kept in the city. Thereafter, he administrated a small parish, St. Monica's, in town, keeping on the right side of the right people, seeing everything, keeping quiet, hating it subconsciously. "Only now after all I have been through;" he thought, "I can admit. I hated it."

His breakdown had come the first Sunday after Christmas, on the tenth year after his inauguration. He had begun saying the service and as he stood on the altar, his two arms stretched out, he had moved his mouth but no sound had come. Two members of the congregation had come and taken him away.

It had seemed to him as if it was happening to someone else. He had listened outside himself while the psychiatrists had tested and probed and asked questions to which they got no answers. And then, slowly he had slipped back into his body again to face the anguish and confusion that he knew was lying in wait.

The psychiatrists had left him alone after a while. He was not violent. He just refused to speak. Then someone had come and told him his mother was dying. It was the first time he had listened to another human voice in three months.

"I do not want to see her," he had said.

The psychiatrists had rejoiced. The shock, they maintained, had brought him back.

Still, he had been taken to see his mother. She had been ill, it seemed, for a long time and he had not known. As he had sat by the bed watching her, he had kept feeling at bay.

Then his mother had opened her eyes and had seen him.

"My son," she had whispered. "What have they done to you?" He couldn't answer. His eyes blurred with tears. They took him away.

A week later she had died in her sleep. When they told him, he had not shed a tear. That day he had asked to see the Bishop.

The Bishop had entered the room, his fat pink face beaming.

"Ah! My son, you are looking much better I must say."

"Your Excellency, l want to leave the church."

The Bishop had looked startled at the suddenness of this request. But all he had said was:

"I'll give you some time to think it over."

They had sent him to teach at Cucumber Bank. It was so remote that he would have time, they had said, to reflect on the wisdom of his decision. He did not mind. He had wanted to breathe fresh air again and rejoice everyday, away from all those memories. "Now I am here. I do not even want to remember that I was a priest. I will never be one again." Still, thinking about the past made his heart heavy and weighed down his spirits. He quickened his pace, forcing himself to think about something else.

Teacher arrived at school cheered by the sound of children's voices shouting across the yard. He had grown accustomed to their happy sound. Even on a morning like this one, when the unaccustomed and unwanted memories had intruded like an unwelcome guest, they made him feel secure and calm again. He went to the desk and rang the bell.

The children trooped inside the thatched building whispering and giggling, and sat down on their benches.

"Good morning children," he said.

"Good mawnin' Teecha," they chorussed.

Just then he heard a commotion by the door. He saw a red-eyed Miss Maisie standing there, looking agitated. He then remembered that her father was dying and he immediately went to meet her.

"Teecha, Pa dead."

"Oh, I am sorry to hear that. Do you want to sit down?"

"No tenks Teecha ah haffe go mek arrangements. Ah jus' mi wah know if since no parson de, if you could do di burial?"

He couldn't breathe, it seemed. He stared at her, surprised. Then the full meaning of her request penetrated his brain.

It was that first Sunday again.

He was again in church. All around him there were tall red candles glowing in the big cathedral. There was the scent of fresh pine from the green tree that the parishioners had decorated so beautifully for Midnight Mass the week before. He was at the altar again his two hands outstretched to begin the mass and his mouth was opening and closing soundlessly... two men from the parish were lifting him up taking him away.

With great effort of will he forced himself to breathe normally, to focus himself and to come back to the white-washed plastered wall of the school. He was trembling.

"Teecha?" Miss Maisie's voice came sharply to him. She had noticed his agitation.

He couldn't do as she asked. He wasn't yet ready to face his ghosts again. Suppose he blacked out like that time?

"All Teecha?" she repeated anxiously.

He nodded his head, not trusting himself to speak. Then as from afar he heard his own voice answering quietly.

"Yes, of course. What time should I be there?"

Miss Maisie left soon after, having other arrangements to make.

Teacher's mind was in a turmoil. His thoughts were constantly on the ordeal ahead. Why had he jeopardised his carefully constructed peace of mind? He needed time to compose himself. Quickly he made a decision.

"Jacob," he told a student, "call all the teachers to my office please."

When all the teachers were assembled, he announced. "As there will be a burial at three today and I will be officiating, I will be declaring a holiday and sending the children home. Please dismiss your classes."

No one said anything. The teachers seemed to sense that something was wrong. Quietly they left. In a short space of time, the school yard was empty and there was silence.

Teacher sat at his desk and buried his head in his hands feeling his control crumbling as the memories came crowding in. "Teecha!" he heard a soft voice from the doorway. Shaking his head to clear it, he saw that it was Miss Celia who lived about two miles upriver from the school.

"Yes, Miss Celia, please... please come in."

"Teecha, yu yer sey Mista Ramsey dead no? Well, me and Miss Rosie and Mrs. Parham mi di wonder if we could pick some song to practise fi di funeral."

She waited anxiously for his approval. Teacher was amazed. He knew she had just had a stillborn baby two weeks before and here she was offering to prepare a choir for the funeral! But then, death was important to these people. It was a time for supporting the bereaved. Still, he felt he should protest.

"Miss Celia," he began, "are you sure you snould be out like this so soon after having your child?"

She laughed.

"Cho Teecha, me strong yu know. Afta me help sew burying clothes las' night. How me mek latta johnny cake and fry fish fi eat dis evening afterwards." She continued:

Zoila Ellis

"You know Teecha sometime we quarrel 'mongst weself ya da dis village, but when important ting like death happen, everybody pitch in because that could happen to all ah we. Da so we haffe live. We cyan be selfish. When the ribba raise i flood out all ah we. When i good like now, all ah we ketch fish from it fi eat, so jus' like dat we haffe live. If you do someting bad, yu know yu haffe mek it up befo de nex' rainy season because when flood comes, dah da same somebody might haffe help yu save yu life. If somebody do you something bad, well, you haffe try not to hold malice an' have bad heart because yu an' da person might well haffe share di same roof if one a unu house wash weh. Da so we see it."

She paused for breath. It had been a long speech for she was normally a quiet person.

Teacher sensed that the death had caused her to think about her own child that had died. Yet here she was, willing to give and not be brought down. She had lived by the river and she had learnt life's lessons from its hands. He felt humbled. With a lift of spirit he brought out a hymnbook, dusted it carefully and handed it to her.

"Miss Celia, I think yours is a wonderful idea. I'm sure your lovely voice will grace the service."

She smiled shyly and left with a quick thank you, unused to praise.

After she left, it was easy for him to concentrate on the preparation of the service and what he would say. He didn't stop to think of why this was so, he was so grateful for it.

The burial was short and well attended. As he closed the service he felt the tension leave him. Nothing had happened. All he felt was a deep tiredness. The villagers congratulated him on his speech. The men warmly shook his hand. The women offered him johnny cake and fish.

After the burial he visited Miss Bella and her family, not

yet wanting to be alone, still unable to sort out why he felt that something important had happened. Mr. Mangar had gone outside to tie up the horses. The children were sitting around the kitchen table doing their homework by the pale yellow glow of the kerosene lantern.

He and Miss Bella were sitting in the parlour facing a huge vase of red plastic roses.

Unbidden, his voice broke the quiet.

"I used to be a priest you know."

"True Teecha? What happen? Yu stop?"

"Yes, I stopped."

"Oh well, betta yu stop something than yu eena it with only half yu hart."

After that, silence again. She had not asked him about it. To her, it did not matter, he felt. Here, he was Teacher. Somewhere else, he had been a priest, but he had stopped. Suddenly, he felt like hugging her but all he said was "I must go now. It is getting dark. The day has been a long one. Please say goodbye to your husband for me."

"O.K. Teecha," she replied.

He went down to where he had tied his small boat, got in and cast off, dipping his paddle gently in the river. As he paddled home, he felt like laughing and crying at the same time. How could she know what she had done for him? Her simplicity and truth were as natural as the river and together they had set him free.

ab Seasin

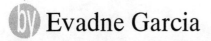 from *A Child Remembers*

by Evadne Garcia

*T*odeh, Bilize City nuh stan like ih mih stan when wih dah mih pickney. Deh nevah gah no Bella Vista, all dehm pretty house deh, an dah king's Pahk mih nevah dih deh atahl. Dih city mih ehn right dah Fabah's Road junkshan. Dih Westan Highway mih nevah gah no light, an all who mi waahn waatah an mih nevah gah vat eenah deh yaad mih hafih guh dah stan-pipe[1].

Laahd, dih line suh lang, suhm bring dehn waatah bucket pahn kyaat, and eenah May, dih pipe hihn jus dih 'drip-drip.' While dehn gial dih 'shush', we bwoy dih play cowbwoy, maable or caparuche[2].

When dih Aagass rain finish, dih whole a Bilize City aandah waatah. Well, as wih mih dih deh pahn haliday, wih dicide fih guh ketch crab. Dih bes place fih mih ketch crab dehn dah mih up Fabah's Road. Billy, Jahn and 'Spegle' seh dehm mih gwine wid mih. Nuh badah fih try ketch crab if yuh nuh gah yuh crab ketching 'tools'.

Yuh mus have hook, crocus beg an wahn kis-kis[3]. Me? ah gah home gahn beg Ma fih len mih ih kis-kis. Sean seh hihn wah bring in Grampa crocus beg dehm. Wih mek wih hook frahn wah piece a close-line weh wih fine eenah Miss

Mary yaad. Wih lef tung roun ten a'clack. Now evri-bady know dat dih bes time fih ketch crab dah bitween ten dah mahning and two dah aftahnoon. Dis time dih waatah eenah dih hole dih bile; dehn kyaahn stay eenah deh, dehn hafl cuhm out pahn dih road! Wih waahk slow up Fabah's Road, evri way wih look wih sih crab-hole and crab...

Wehn wih pass Misah Coco Tee house, wih staat to ketch crab. Spegle dah dih fus wahn fih ketch wahn lee, chinchi crab. Dehn, evri-bady gahn crazy-crab fih days! Sudden wih heah Sean shout, "Bwoy, unuh cuhm yah, a sih wahn big bo. Dis wahn fih mih todeh; todeh, dis big clah gwine eenah soup".

Billy seh, "Hook ah bwoy, Sean hook ahm".

Sean call back, "Sumbady, bring dih kis-kis mek wih grab ah pahn ih back."

Me?, I open ih crocus beg. Dis time, Sean pin dih crab an ih mi wah put ah eenah ih crocus beg wehn wih heah Jahn staat to laaf like ih simple.

"Ha, ha, ha, Sean bwoy, dah weh duh yuh? Yuh hafi let dah wahn guh."

"Yuh crazy or wat bwoy?... Dis dah dih biggis crab weh wih ketch todeh!", Sean seh.

Now Jahn kyaahn hole up, "Sean, yuh nuh sih dah Wash Palm[4] yuh gah deh? Wih kyaahn ker dat home."

Now evri-bady look pahn dah big brute good, dehn Billy ans Spegle really staat tuh laaf fih troo. Yuh sih, Wash Palm crab gah ih egg pahn ih belly an dehn nuh tase nice. Sean mih really waahn dah crab, but it letih guh. Bout wahn-turty suh dih aftahnoon, wih mih gah at least ten crab each, suh wih decide fih guh home.

Dis time, wih waahk dung dih Westan Highway frahm the junkshan. Wehn wih reach dehm Indian pipple house, Jahn hihn decide fih guh get blackberries. All a wih gahn up eenah dih tree an put Spegle fih watch fih Miss Rancharan.

Chuh, wehn wih staat tuh pick an eat ripe blackberry, nobady memebah she. Dis nex ting wih no, she stan up right andah dih berry tree... wid ih mule-whip eenah ih han!

Limb, branch an man scattah, dung dih road; only Jahn mih lef up eenah dih tree. Dih las ting wih yerri, dah ole Miss Rancharan dih seh, "A ketch wahn ah unuh now, unuh lee brute. Yuh hafi cuhm dung an ah wah wait right yah fih yuh." Nobady look back, nobady stap – suhtay with reach Laahd's Ridge Cimitry. Nobady mih wah be dih fus or las fih guh eenah an lef deh!

Ten minits aftah wih reach Grampa house, wih sih Jahn dih cuhm. Ih seh. "Dih nex time unuh ruhn lef mih, a gwine tell Miss Rancharan dat dah yuh Billy, Sean and Clive, unuh mih foce mih fih climb ih berries tree."

Mah sen wih gahn bie treeh pung a coco, wahn cucnat an foah green plaantin. Dah nite, wih eat lattah crab soup, wid plenty a Matilda foot[5].

Glassary

1 stan-pipe	Waatah facit fih dih hole ah dih villige.
2 caparuche	Pickney playting, wahn tap weh mek outtah wahn piece ah wood, ih shape like wahn cone an ih gah wahn nail inside. Fih spin ah, ih gah wahn lang string weh fix pahn wahn battle stappah.
3 kis-kis	'U' shape holdah weh mek outtah 'Puck-O-Nuh-Bwoy' treeh. Ih use fih hole hat coal pahn dih fiah-haath.
4 Wash Palm	Laydih crab wid ih egg outside, pahn ih belly.
5 Matilda foot	Dumplin frahm gratah green plantin, saal an ile.

ird Wish

 Among my Souvenirs

by Lawrence G. Vernon

*T*he old man turned the dark green, almost opaque stone over and over in his hand then looked questionably up at his son.

"What is it, Jim?"

"That's jade, dad." Jim Hilton answered. "It's a common enough stone, but this one is extra special. See those carvings on it?"

Old Mr. Hilton looked at the stone, which was flat and round about the size of a half dollar. There was a hole bored on one edge as if it was meant to be worn like a medallion. He pushed his glasses a little higher on his nose and looked carefully at the stone again. He did make out some lines cut into it, and as he followed the outlines with the finger of one hand a very grinning and grotesque face took form. It apparently was not meant to be either man or animal, but rather some being not yet created, or some hideous thing seen only in the minds of the mad and the evil.

"What is it, son?" the old man asked again, passing it to his wife, Sarah, in the nearby chair. "I have never seen a stone like that before, and that picture on it..."

"It's supposed to be a magic stone." Jim was standing near to his mother looking at the stone with her. He had just come down for the weekend from a site some American archaeologists were excavating a few miles out of the city. Just under thirty, Jim was the government's expert on excavating old Mayan sites. "I have seen a picture of it before," he continued. "In a book one of the men loaned me. Apparently they had found a similar one four years ago in a ruin in Guatemala. You see, the old Mayas built up an amazing civilization during the 9th century or so. They didn't know of any metals so they had to use stone tools to shape their buildings. After a while this great civilization just faded. There are many theories why this happened, but we won't go into that. These Mayas were very ceremonial and superstitious in their beliefs, and this book I had tells of a strange legend about that stone you have there."

Jim then related a story which could have been something from a fairy tale. Only three of the jade stones were known to have been cut by an old Maya priest who practiced sorcery. He imbued these stones with the power of granting three wishes to the owner. The book only recorded what happened to the owner of one of the stones. He seems to have used his power to kill his enemies, so the priest punished him. He suffered so much that he used his last wish in asking for death. The stone passed through several generations and all its owners died violently. At last someone buried it to get rid of it and its evil powers, and it must have been only Jim's hand that held it since then. The book had even gone so far as to say that any person who found it would be granted the usual three wishes, and mentioned what they were.

"What are they?" asked his father.

"I would never use those three wishes dad, and I will never tell anyone. I should have left the stone where it was or buried it again. If the legend is true, which I have no way of knowing, it is an evil stone, and if not, well, why take chances."

"But you kept it. You brought it home."

"Yes because I thought I might show a few friends, but I reconsidered on my way home and decided to get rid of it. I am not afraid to tell you now that I am afraid of it."

His father took back the stone and looked at it, rubbing his thumb gently over the smooth surface. If he could wish he would ask for money. They would all be rich, and the mortgage on the house could be paid. But Jim would not consent.

Jim's voice cut into his thoughts. "Well, I'm pretty tired and it's late. Better take a rest." He extended his hand for the stone, dropped it into a small paper bag and went to his room after saying goodnight to his parents.

The old man lay awake long that night, thinking that there would certainly be no harm in keeping the stone, making just one wish, then getting rid of it. But Jim was too cautious, almost a coward. Now if he was Jim and had found the stone... The temptation was too great and he couldn't stand the thought of having the stone re-buried, of losing something so valuable.

He got out of bed silently, went to his drawer and searched until he found a silver medal he had earned in the first World War. He removed the ribbon, and holding the medal tightly in his hands, crept silently out of his room into Jim's. Jim was always a sound sleeper, so it was no problem to locate the paper bag on his table, remove the jade stone and replace it with the medal. There was hardly any fear of Jim opening the bag again after the way he spoke last night.

Sunday passed and Jim had gone back to work on Monday morning, when Mr. Hilton got the stone from his room, showed it to his wife, and told her what he had done. It was quite natural to tell her, because they had shared so much together, and this was a little thing. She was taken back, almost scared at first, but he spoke to her and reasoned with her until she could practically see the mortgage on their house being paid. They didn't want more than that. They were fairly comfortable, and if the mortgage could be taken from over their heads they could live out the rest of their lives in security.

Two hours passed, however, before Mr. Hilton gathered the courage to make his wish. It seemed so stupid of him to be making wishes like in fairy tales. Those things were only of the imagination. He locked himself in his room so that no one could observe him, took the piece of jade in his hand and wished. He wished, to what or to who, he didn't know, for four thousand dollars. He didn't know what to do after that. Would the money suddenly appear on the bed. Or would a voice whisper to him where to find it?

Five minutes passed and he began to have second thoughts over this stupidness. A grown man, past sixty, making wishes to a stone. He looked at it in his palm, and the face leered back at him as if in mockery. He threw it on the bed in disgust and stalked from the room, not so much in anger as in frustration.

That night he couldn't sleep well again, and lay thinking a long time. Maya legends were as they were called, he concluded – legends. No one really believed them, but he supposed he had clutched at the straw Jim had flung before him like any ordinary man would have. He had made himself believe that he could get money, that he could give a lie to legends.

The next morning he was miserable from lack of sleep, and blaming the jade for his discomfort and childish belief, made a mental note to get rid of it later in the day. By this time Jim would have missed it anyhow, and might be coming back. The knock on the front door came as he was pulling out his chair for breakfast, and he looked at his wife across the table. Jim must have come back already. It was quite early for visitors, and the old man's mind raced wildly trying to figure his next move.

His hands released the chair and he walked to the door as the knocking sounded again. A stranger confronted him. A foreigner from his looks. He asked for Mr. Hilton, and declined the old man's invitation to enter. He got to the point of his visit right away, and from the table where she was seated Mrs. Hilton could hear most of what he was saying. An accident had occurred at the excavation site where Jim was working. Jim had been crushed to death by rocks which had worked loose from a partly unearthed pyramid. They were trying to dig him out now, but he was buried rather deeply, and they were not sure how long it would take. They regretted the accident, and would like to offer Jim's parents a modest sum of money, which the company knew could not commensurate for the loss of their son's life, but which might help the couple in some small way.

Mr. Hilton did not say anything as the man handed him a cheque and left. He stared at it blankly, turned into the room and went over to comfort his wife who was weeping loudly. The old man was wondering how money could take the place of their son. How could four thousand dollars ever...

Four thousand dollars! The same amount he had wished for. Exactly four thousand dollars! Was it simply by coincidence it had happened that way, or was it a morbid way of answering his wish? No, he did not want it that way. Jim was too good to go so cheaply.

The thought knawed at the old man's conscience for two weeks, while his wife mourned and fretted. She had hardly spoken until a few days ago when she seemed to have developed an idea. She had thought of a way of using the stone again, but her husband would not agree. She had pleaded with him to wish their son alive again. Had he not got his first wish? One of the things she loved most in life was gone forever. Now there was the possibility of bringing it back. It surely could hurt nobody to try.

But the old man kept silent. The idea awed him. That a piece of green stone could be used to restore life to a dead body. Impossible. He had become more and more convinced over the days though that the stone, that evil face on the stone, had something to do with the death of their boy. He could not understand and his aged mind could not reason with itself anymore. All he knew was that he had wished for money and his boy had died. The most he could do was to let him lie in peace.

His wife slowly pined away day by day, and eventually he feared that she might die also. He would make the wish to please her, and hope that the stone was in reality a farce. He might be able to prove to her that it could not possibly have any effect on their lives.

That day he made the wish. It was near on to midnight, and they were sleeping soundly when a knocking on the front door awoke them. Mr. Hilton sat up in bed as the knocking continued, and even in his half-sleeping condition he detected a familiarity in the knocking. It was a guarded rap-rapping as if the person did not want to knock very loudly to disturb the neighbors. The way Jim always knocked when he came down from work late.

His wife had detected the same thing and was busy getting out of bed. He turned on the light as her emaciated body moved swiftly out of the bedroom towards the front door where the knocking was getting more persistent. He heard her saying, "It's my boy, it's my boy." And he did not move. If the magic stone had granted his wish again and brought back Jim, or his ghost, he was not sure what condition the body would be in. They were not allowed to see what was left of Jim after they dug him out, and he was sure his wife could not stand the sight of her once fine son, perhaps crushed beyond recognition. After all he had not wished for his son as he was in life. He had only wished him alive. No. He could not let his wife see beyond that door.

He hurriedly reached in his drawer, and his fingers felt the cold stone of the jade just as he heard the key turn loudly in the lock of the front door. His lips moved frantically as he uttered the third and final wish.

The knocking stopped immediately and he stood still for a few seconds, listening. Wondering if he was in time. Then he walked from the room into the parlor and saw his wife holding the door wide open, looking from side to side. As he reached the open door he saw that the light from the lamp-post across the street showed a quiet and deserted street.

He locked the door and gently led his wife back inside, pleased that his third wish had been granted.

7

The

ay of the Bridge

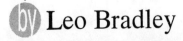 *from* *Belizean Flavour*

by Leo Bradley

*J*ackie Dean knew it would happen some day. But when it did, he of all people had to be involved.

Jackie was a pensive, Belize City born youth of seventeen. "You dream too much" his folks always told him. But Jackie did not care about this slur. One could call him an introvert if he wanted, but when he drew himself into his interior thoughts, many feelings of delight took flame, and some were right after all. And now for several days came the same anticipation. That same, complacent, dependable Belize City Swing Bridge which everyone took for granted, would go on strike some day. This thought revived again and again in Jackie's mind.

And so it did.

People ignored that Swing Bridge too much. After all, the Belize City Swing Bridge (over fifty years old and the victim of two massive hurricanes) and its ancestors have conveyed ever so many across the dark, sluggish Belize River. They gave passage to my father and grandfather, and probably yours too. We should give its solid form and features a little thought sometime.

The Belize Swing Bridge stretches its flat form across

the stream to reach on one side the squatting Fire Station and a wharf, and on the other, the crowded fish, meat and fruit historic Central Market and a wharf. Day in and day out pass the constant procession of pedestrians, vehicles, bicycles, carts, and what not. Below it glide the doreys, put-putting bum boats and skiff power boats. And above it the solitary sea gull or man-of-war bird wings silently towards the sea. Methodically in the early morning and late afternoon, there are the two official swingings of the bridge. One Belizean off to war duty mentions that he was checked for security purposes by being asked the times when the Belize Swing Bridge was swung.

What tales that bridge could tell if it only broke its silence! There would be tales of market chatters and sailors' savory curses, gossips of pedestrians and the revelry of parades – even whisperings of the lonely, despondent soul peering into the dark river water to unload dull thoughts.

Yes, people took this bridge for granted. When it was swung two times daily officially, or for emergency swingings, labourers with back-breaking toil would twist its central control; and its form would turn parallel to the stream to allow barges and boats to pass from the wharves and dock-yards or out to sea. When this occurred, Belize City was practically cut in half. People of all classes and sizes waited at either end for its return. New convertibles and the latest in cars and trucks, vehicles of yesteryear, bicycles, people, baby carriages, buses and more people all assembled in orderly fashion to await its return to duty. "How powerful and important I am!" the old mass of steel and cement thought; "I must give service for such meek obedience!"

But people got complacent at its dependable, regular efficiency. Yes, familiarity breeds contempt. So thought our

Belize City Swing Bridge; and then it chuckled with delight. A wicked thought began lurking way down its bosom of steel. Perhaps it was mental telepathy that brought the same message to dreamy Jackie.

The trouble is that Jackie had to be involved. Here it is how it all happened.

It was a calm, clear evening in late May – one of those Belizean evenings when, after a warm day, the golden globe of sunset drops hazily behind the cemetery swamps. Jackie left his Racecourse Street home hurriedly. And why not! He was bound for a matinee show at a Queen Street cinema where he was to meet Flora. Flora was a young dream-girl he had met at a highschool fair. Flora had non-committally said she would be at the matinee. So Jackie was attired in typical, sporting Belize youth clothing. This included a flashy tee-shirt, dark blue Jeans, set off with one of the expensive varieties of white tennis shoe. Of course there was the dangling, gold chain with black coral pendant, and a digital watch. And Jackie was a little handsome at that! This all added up to make by-standers watch the youth, as he hurried on down Albert Street for his appointment. He had no time to gaze. His mind and heart were at the Queen Street cinema.

Then as he passed by Central Square, he observed people and vehicles hurrying towards the Swing Bridge. Jackie knew he had to race for it. And of course he was not alone. Last minute pedestrians were already in a hundred yards dash, hoping to get across before the swinging of the bridge. Even a few bicycle riders were stretching the rope to speed across.

Jackie even ignored the policeman as he raced for the bridge. He could not afford to be late. But what luck! Now he was stranded on the bridge. His disappointed mind could hardly pay attention to the steady whine as the labourers twisted the levers, pushing the bridge further out. Neither could he hear the occasional jeers of youths at either end as they observed this solitary maroon stranded on the bridge form. What a predicament. All the uncertainty of unsettled youth summoned up itself into his teeming head. It had to happen to him, Jackie Dean, on the very day he might be lucky. What dirty, miserable, embarrassing luck!

At that very time old Mr. Bridge was chuckling to himself. This would be the day he would refuse to budge. This was his day. As the men put down their levers, and the bridge rode to a stop in mid-stream, he prepared himself to stay put. He tightened his joints, flexed his muscles; and decided that this time he would not move when the men tried to turn him in. He relaxed complacently as a wide, cargo barge crept up towards the passageway, pulled by a tug boat. It was moving too fast, and there was scarcely any lee-way as the barge slanted a little. Alas, while Mr. Bridge was relaxing and Jackie was excited, the barge accidentally gave the bridge a massive, jolting blow. Well, this certainly jammed the bridge indeed, and whether he wanted to return to the shore or not, Mr. Bridge could not move! He had hoped to tantalize Belizeans for a while, but now Mr. Bridge was really stuck.

Up went an unanimous shout from the people, and others came to watch as the barge was swiftly pulled through the passageway. But little did the on-lookers realize that the barge had done a dirty deed to Mr. Bridge. When all the boats had passed, and the workers re-commenced working the bridge back to the shore, it would not move. It was properly jammed in centre-stream.

Jackie peered over the side at the river; threw away his cigarette; looked at his watch; looked at it again; decided to give the workers a help at the levers; then realized that he was stranded indeed. The great concourse of people were joined by many more. Gradually the atmosphere of curiosity and entertainment gave way to one of impatience – impatience of tired workers wanting to get home, strollers wishing to get to their destination, traffic jam and a solitary, confused youth wanting to meet his girl. But poor Mr. Bridge was stuck solidly. And try as hard as they could, the workers could not move him. And now all along the waterfront, from market people, fishermen, worried people and inquisitive youngsters, steady gazes and running remarks filled the air, including political remarks. Impatient workers shouted all sorts of advice. "Do this! Do that! Turn backwards then forwards, but hurry up, man." These and other less recordable remarks flew right and left. The workers tried and tried but with no luck.

The city lights had gone on. All Belize City, it seemed, had congregated by the bridge; and despondent Jackie, anxious and frustrated, had given up all hopes of getting to the matinee. The Belize Swing Bridge stood still, swingless. Then up came officials, pulled from their supper. Even the bridge tried his best. But it was stuck much. A few bystanders crossed the river in doreys; and this started a brisk business with dorey owners. Jackie almost missed his step when he tried unsuccessfully to get into one.

Then ropes were attached to either end of the bridge; and trucks on the shore pulled in unison from Northside and Southside. But there was no success, at least not at first. It was almost after two hours of trial and error when Mr. Swing Bridge, budged by a combination of ropes, muscles, boat ends, etc., limped slowly back to starting position.

Jackie was almost crushed unconscious as the flowing mass of humanity surged from north and south to negotiate the way across the bridge, not to mention the procession of delayed vehicles. When he was pushed steadily out to Queen Street, and the sleek, well-dressed appearance of Jackie was gone, the cinema show was also finished.

Again he moved dejectedly towards the unfriendly bridge for home. As he passed the car-park by Central Square, his heart jumped as he saw Flora walking with a friend of his. She shouted casually at him.

"Well, a mi wait fu yu, sap!"

"But di bridge mi di act badders!"

"The bridge?"

"Yes, i mi stuck."

"Why yu mi have to cross di bridge? A sure we mi agree fi meet da Palace. Yu lose out, boy!"

Now how do you like that! Jackie had to learn that at times girls can be a little less predictable than the old swing bridge. Jackie stood speech-less as Flora went off with a mere wave of her hand. His clothes were as rumpled as his mind. There went all the effort, and patience, and anticipation. Jackie turned back nonchalantly, wandering once more over the bridge. And as he dragged himself by the pedestrian side of the bridge, he peered into the black stream where moon-beams were playing near to fishing boats. And if old Mr. Swing Bridge could talk, it could say too what feverish thoughts were welling up in Jackie's mind, and what frustrating words he was whispering. The day of the bridge had turned into a night of desperation for him.

gar

from *Pataki Full*

by Colville Young

Old Tio Diego lived in a tiny hut on the edge of town. It was away from the roadside and dwarfed by great bukut trees that grew nearby. Smaller trees and shrubs around the hut made it difficult for it to be seen from the road.

The hut was the smallest in the town, so small it didn't seem possible any living being outside of Grimm's Tales could live in it.

But Tio Diego lived in it, all alone. He was a small, wizened old man – small like his home. His wrinkled skin was the same colour as the thatch, brittle with great age, which formed the roof of the hut. His limbs were so bony, so delicate, you felt as if you would break him by just touching him except with the greatest gentleness, as if he had shrivelled to only a fraction of what he had been as a young man when the red life-bearing blood had coursed joyously through his body.

And Tio Diego was poor, absolutely destitute. Yet for a poor man, he did a very curious thing every morning. Come to think of it now, it is surprising that it could ever have come to be taken for granted, but such was the case.

People had just stopped noticing or even realizing that

Sugar

Tio Diego every morning left his tiny hut on the edge of town, limped anciently to San Riverol's restaurant near the park in the center of town, and ordered and paid for a breakfast.

True, it was the cheapest breakfast money could buy: black coffee, a few tortillas or two slices of bread, a dab of fried beans... Still, every poor man knows it is always cheaper to prepare one's meal than to buy it at a restaurant – even at San Riverol's where prices were, as advertised on the wall, 'barato, muy barato'.

But long ago everyone had stopped remarking how mysterious it was that a viejito who only made a handful of coppers a day selling firewood (or bukuts and craboos when they were in season) should be eating at a restaurant like that.

Maybe everyone just came to accept it as one of those unaccountable eccentricities of old age.

Then one morning the mystery was solved. Just as Tio Diego had finished his breakfast, wiped his white-bristled chin with the back of his hand and begun limping through the door, Juanita, San's assistant, leaned over and whispered fiercely in San's ear.

"Are you sure, Juanita?" San asked when his pretty assistant paused for a breath.

"Sure I'm sure!" snapped the other. "Don't you always tell me how my eyes are sharp?"

"And your tongue – but that is another matter."

"Look, keep your remarks less personal", spat out Juanita. Then, "Do I run behind the old rascal?"

"No-o-o", said San Riverol slowly. "Let's wait till tomorrow. I want to watch this thing for myself."

"But he won't if you are watching", argued Juanita.

"He won't know I'm watching", pointed out San.

"We've got the advantage of him now; we know what he's doing but he doesn't know we know."

"He's been having the advantage for a long time now, years and years", said Juanita. Suddenly she giggled uncontrollably. "But what an idea! Jesus! Maria! What an idea, man!"

Then she saw San Riverol's humourless face and controlled her giggles, coughing and sputtering in the process.

The next morning, San watched as he had planned. Then after old Tio Diego had finished eating and wiped his mouth, had paid carefully, grudgingly, cent by cent, and was making for the door, San's voice rang out.

"Just a moment, Señor Diego." At the sound, as if by magic the old man's footsteps quickened; the limp was now just a trace.

As the footsteps of the departing customer quickened, San Riverol set out behind him.

At this point the old man saw flight was useless and slowed down. He pretended he was walking normally – in fact, that everything was normal.

A small crowd, sensing a developing drama as idlers around a village square or town park always will, was beginning to gather.

San addressed this crowd as much as the old man.

"See! See! Every morning for the last I-don't-know-how-many years, this venerable thief come in here and say he buy breakfast. But meanwhile, what the old scamp really doing?" He paused, his sense of drama rising to the occasion. Then he pointed at the old man and said, "thieving my sugar off the restaurant table, sliding nearly a cupful into a paper-bag then sneaking the bag into his dirty pocket. The man take every day more than the value he leave for the breakfast!"

Sugar

Tio Diego had stopped trying to look normal under the amused scrutiny and jeers of the still-gathering crowd. The mask he now wore was one of indignation to cover his embarrassment. He tried to speak, to protest, but his quaverings were drowned by the angry, louder voice of the restaurant proprietor.

"See how he so old and advantageous! By now he must have backed out a barrelful, three – God in his heaven know how many!"

"You question the honesty of a man old enough to be your father?" quavered Tio Diego ineffectually.

"Look", San appealed to the onlookers, "tell him to pull out his pockets. Just tell him that. I see him thief my sugar, see him with my own two eyes."

The old man was beginning to walk away. There were tears of shame, or anger, or both, glistening in the shrunken hollows where his eyes hid themselves behind the prominent cheekbones.

Then suddenly, San seemed to see Tio Diego for the first time. It was as if he had never before been conscious of those small, wrinkled, bony, delicate limbs, of that pitiful quavering voice.

As Tio Diego walked away, it had been San Riverol's intention to walk behind, to insist that the old man pull out his grimy pockets in the presence of the grinning witnesses. Not to press legal charges, perhaps, but (as he put it to himself) to teach him a lesson. But now he suddenly was reminded of his own father, long since dead in his eightieth year; and who knew? the old man before could be an image of himself after fifty years. He turned abruptly and walked back to his restaurant.

That night he filled the biggest paper-bag he could find in the restaurant with sugar and, just before closing time, gave it to Juanita. Refusing any explanation, he ordered her to take it to the little hut on the edge of town and give it to Tio Diego. Half an hour later, Juanita was back.

Then ten minutes later, just as San was bolting the front door, there was a knock. He opened the door. Wordlessly, Tio Diego limped in, put in the bag of sugar on the counter and, controlling the quaver in his voice, said, "Keep your bloody sugar, Señor Riverol."

Then the old man limped out and was swallowed up in the darkness outside. San stood there drumming with his fingers on the counter.

Suddenly Juanita laughed. San whirled angrily on the red lips split to show the even white teeth gleaming in mockery, the eyes lined with too much mascara gleaming in the yellow light of the electric bulb. After Tio Diego's defiant act of dignity and pride, the girl's laugh was very like sacrilege. San glared at her.

"The bag!" gasped Juanita, unable to speak properly, her voice half-smothered with laughter.

"What is it?" snapped San irritably, his eyes following Juanita's pointing finger. For answer, Juanita took up the bag at which she had been pointing and rested it on the restaurant scale. The red needle sped around and quivered to a stop.

"Nearly a pound less. He took out nearly a pound then bring it back so righteously!" She was almost doubled with laughter.

"I always said your eyes are too sharp," grunted San angrily. "Shut your mouth, shut the shop and go home."

Too surprised and puzzled to answer, Juanita did as she had been ordered. After her brass-buckled shoes had clip-clopped out of the shop, San closed the door, bolted it, and stood there a long while, thinking, drumming with his fingers on the counter.

Sugar

For him, Juanita's latest discovery had not detracted from the new dignity he saw in the old man. Instead, the whole wide world was tinged with a new measureless sadness. There was sadness in the fact that there were persons like Juanita who would never be able to understand certain things; sadness in the destruction of Tio Diego's precarious hand-to-mouth existence; even sadness in the fact that San Riverol was a wealthy restauranteur who had never needed, really needed, a pound of sugar.

tter-Sweet
Revenge
from Among my Souvenirs

 John A. Walter

*H*e was the biggest man I have seen – Ripford Harper was.

He stood six feet seven, the feet of his trousers rolled up just below the knees, wearing shirt-sleeves and a small chef's barret at right angle on his semi-triangular head from under which thick, short cropped hair protruded. His hands, incredibly long and hairy dangled awkwardly at his side. He was a perfect picture of a shaved ape, duded up for the late late circus show.

Jack, my brother and I had just arrived in Dovehead and had hurried to the annual post hunting contest barbeque to meet Dad. He had written us so much about the expectations of the villagers of a most wonderful time on this occasion, and had made it sound so interesting, that we just couldn't wait to get there.

Rip Harper, as he was called by everyone, was the hero of the day as he had been on such occasions for over a decade. He had carried away most of the hunting prizes and when Dad took us to his camp, we found him among his souvenirs. Boar's teeth, deer horns, tiger hides and relics of other beasts which had fallen by his hands made up the collections of his 'souvenirs.' There were several camps, each for a hunter. It was an honor to be the invited guest of Rip Harper.

Rip Harper boasted of the finest roast on the whole grounds. He was roasting a large buck over a huge fire, filling the atmosphere with an aroma tantalizing to the nostrils.

"Rip, I want you to meet my boys, Jack and Bernard. They couldn't make it for the hunting contest but here they are for the barbeque." "Fine pair of boys you have Sam. Sorry they missed the hunting fun. Sorry Ma didn't give me two fine bucks instead of those two girls, ha." I took his extended hand and felt a steel clamp clasp my feeble hand. For a while I thought my hand was going to crumble in his. Never was I so glad to end a hand shake.

"I am glad to meet you, Mr. Harper", I said shakily. Jack followed suit and I watched his face changed about three shades of completion before Rip Harper released his grip.

Our host rubbed the palms of his hands together frequently as if excited by something. This, and his regular use of the word 'ha' were peculiar characteristics I could not help to observe. "Why don't you boys take a look around my place? But remember don't touch anything. I will let you in on a little secret of this trade, one touch – the slightest touch of rough hands take years off a deer horn. Go on, look around, ha."

We accepted his invitation and moved inside his tent, looking at his souvenirs. We compared deer horns, boars' teeth and other relics to try to determine which was the most unique. We concluded that a set of boars' teeth about four or five inches long were the best. "A King-Kong even," remarked Jack. "And where are the two girls he sired to his dismay? I bet they look like Annabella, the old hog that does our laundry at the campus."

"Four bits say you are wrong," I challenged.

"A bet, dear brother."

"See those two pert chics approaching from the rostrum, another two bits say they are Rip Harper's daughters."

"What! You lack imagination, dear brother Slim," (My brother calls me Slim causing others to do likewise. I am not slim but he says I remind him of Slim Pickings – ha), he said in his flowery language. "An I hate like the dickings to relieve you of your petty allowances so effortlessly, but because of your numbskullity, I have no alternative but to accept your additional bet."

The two girls came towards the tent, then went towards Dad who was watching Rip Harper barbequing his deer. Jack and I followed them.

"You girls having a wonderful time, ha?" inquired Rip Harper.

"Oh, yes, Pa," they replied together.

"Hey fellas," called Rip Harper looking up seeing us, "come over here and meet my daughters Joanie and Sylvia. These here are Sam Madison's two boys, Jack and Bernard."

The hand shaking was a contrast to those with their father. Later I collected six bits from Jack which he paid ruefully.

Sylvia was the younger of the two girls, about my age. She was also the more lovelier. Her body was perfect. A masterpiece sculpture, moulded by the hands of an infinite artist. A masterpiece indeed! Her hazel brown hair was fascinatingly illuminated by the low glow of the barbeque's fire. Her smile which was disarming, went directly where she sent it to your heart and places beyond. Her eyes, oh what lovely eyes! – How much more they added to her charms!

I talked with her, small talk, and after many awkward

tries and suggestions, I finally came out with an invitation to dance, which she readily accepted. I could not help to steel glances at her lovely profile as we danced. She was a superb dancer. The first few steps were most uncomfortable for me. Our nearness, the coziness of the lights, the suggestion of romance in the atmosphere, and the lovely music did nothing to improve my awkward state. I felt a hard lump forming in my throat and thought I would sound hoarse if ever I attempted to speak. But gradually, as we danced I became more at ease and before a set was through I was really having a wonderful time.

I was very sad when time came for her to go home. All she left me with was a faint promise that we might see each other again. The memories of her loveliness, her charms, her intelligence, were imbedded in my mind. I had to face the fact – I was in love with Sylvia Harper.

Several days had passed and I did not see her. I was not enjoying myself in Dovehead the way I had anticipated, all because of my lovesickness. Then one day, while I was brooding over my lost love, Jack came up to me and said.

"Why the gloomy countenance, dear brother?"

"Do I look gloomy? And if so, what is it to you?", I asked hotly, not being in any mood for any of his wise-cracks.

"Your gloominess protrudes like a sick toe: Boy-ibus see-ibus pretty girl-orum, boy-ibus love-ibus pretty girl-orum, but boy-ibus can't-ibus see-ibus pretty girl-orum."

I kept silent.

"Reticent, eh? And the answer is Sylvia. I am wise, dear brother, so worry no more. Soon you shall see your Sylvia, and thanks to me."

He had something up his sleeves I knew. He always

grins like a cheshire cat whenever he had something up his sleeves.

"Okay, okay, let's hear it," I said.

He said, "I have news for you, dear brother..."

"Well, spill it and for heaven sake, cut out the 'dear brother' bit."

"As you wish, dear brother – you go for the Sylvia kid, right?"

"What is it to you?"

"I go for Joanie too, but in a big way, I must confess."

"Gee, good. So now we know."

"Don't be sarcastic, dear Slim. Tonight you see your Sylvia and thanks to me."

He is a born braggart, I thought.

"Gee thanks a million, dear brother. What do we do, kidnap Rip Harper?"

"Nothing so melodramatic, Slim, I have a simple plan."

"Please don't tell me Jack." I pleaded.

"Huh?" he asked in surprise.

I kept remembering the countless times Jack had gotten me into scraps. And the funny thing about him is that he himself is never caught. I am always the one left holding the bag. A bagaboo. He reminded me of that mythical character of wittism known as brear Annancy, who is famous for his tricks of every conceivable sorts played on other characters and he is never hurt. His motto is two troubles are better than one and what is the use of getting into trouble without being able to get out. And he always gets himself into the most impossible-to-get-out spots and invariably gets out smiling – like Mohamed Ali Clay.

I could never forget the time Jack and I tied an ear of corn to Old Esau's goat horn. The poor beast tried and tried to get the corn which was dangling just above its nose.

After discovering it could not reach the corn, the goat went frantic, fell over a bank side and broke its neck. I was terribly frightened but jack was calm. Just them we saw Old Esau coming along and Jack adopted an atmosphere of vexation.

"Mr. Esau; Sir, Slim and I were just passing through your pasture and look what we found. One of your goats brutally murdered by same sadist. But don't you worry none, Sir, because I am going to find him and when I do I will give him a licking he will never forget." A drop of tear fell from Jack's eye and had I not seen him and actually aided him in his mischievous act, I would have pushed my hands to fire for him.

"Don't worry, son," Old Esau said. "Whoever done it will get his punishment from up yonder." He pointed towards the sky.

Jack was like that!

"Humiliation I can stand," I said.

"Don't you trust me, Slim?"

"Sure I do. Like I trust a practical joker at a gag-party. Only less."

"There is no harm in hearing out my plan, is there?"

"I... I guess not."

"Good. I did a bit of sleuthing around while you were brooding over the fact that you could not see your dame. Both you and I know that Old Rop don't cater to young bucks go fooling around his girls. There is hell to pay to whosoever he catches. There are several stories about what he did to different boys he caught around his place. Like the Mayor's son he caught necking with Joanie in the garden. Gave him a good walloping, he did. And there was not a thing the Mayor could do about it. Peeved he was, but nothing he could do. But then, nobody does anything to Rip Harper in this man's town – just nobody.

"But you and I are city guys. We are smart. Listen, Slim, tonight at eight Rip goes to Cash Burns place to play stud poker. He goes every Wednesday night, and sometimes doesn't return until midnight. So while he is gone we move in. Simple, isn't it?"

"It sounds simple, but suppose he returns suddenly – what then?"

"Suppose Mr. Compose never had any nose... we got to take the chance, boy. Life is made up of chances, or didn't you know?"

"Yeah, I know, but your type of chances usually take a man to his grave."

"Okay, okay. Let's dispense with the 'palabras' and come to a conclusion: Are you going or are you not going?"

A man knows when his is trapped. I was. I knew. I agreed to go along. Apprehension mounted as we waited behind a clump of hibiscus waiting for Rip Harper's departure. He left home at exactly eight o'clock. I was beginning to believe that for once Jack might not get me in any trouble.

We gave him five minutes grace then crossed the street and went into Rip Harper's yard. We climbed the step – Jack moving ahead bravely and me lagging behind, my apprehensions now replaced by a sweet anticipation of seeing Sylvia.

Jack knocked on the door politely. We waited. Presently Joanie opened the door.

"Oh!" she gasped, putting her hand over her mouth.

"Goodnight, my lovely," said Jack. "You are indeed a sight to sour eyes."

"Who is it?" came a voice from within. Sylvia's melodious voice.

"Come see for yourself... Jack, what are you doing here? If Dad should catch you..."

"Have no fear my sweet. But tell me, are you glad to see us?"

"Of course we are," came the simultaneously reply as Sylvia came out a bedroom.

"Good. Aren't you going to invite us within your humble threshold?"

"Yes, do come in." said Sylvia.

We went inside.

The four of us stood looking at each other awkwardly for a few moments not knowing what to say. Then Jack broke the spell.

"Are you girls glad to see us?"

"Of course we are," they replied simultaneously once more.

Jack grinned.

"Why don't you and Sylvia take a walk in the garden, Slim?" he suggested.

"A good idea," I agreed.

"Suits me." said Sylvia.

I took her hands and we walked through the rear door into the garden. The night air was fresh, and a faint scent of chrysanthemums came to my nostrils. The garden was dark, with only the faint glow from the house aiding visibility. We sat on a small bench and talked.

Sylvia's mother died when she was born and her father played the part of father and mother. He had never thought of marrying anyone again, for he loved his daughters too much to trust their care to any other woman who might not treat them the right way.

Maybe half and hour had elapsed and when I held her she came willingly into my arms, our lips met hungrily, sending a thousand thrills into my being beyond imagination. Our embrace lingered when... "Ha, what I have here?" Rip Harper asked.

His hand, like a twenty pound mall rested on my shoulder, its grip gradually tightening. I stood in rigid immobility, not knowing whether to scream or keep silent. I wished the ground would have opened and swallowed me.

"Go to the house, Sylvia. I am gonna teach this brat a lesson he'll never forget."

Sylvia went into the house.

"Sam Madison's boy, ha. Now why in the world would you want to sneek into my premises trying to see my daughter?"

"I... I was only..."

"Was only what? I say you, boy, and when I saw you I could read your thoughts and they were not at all good thoughts."

I wondered about Jack, and felt a tinge of relief knowing that Sylvia would warn him.

"I could give you a good wallop, boy, but I have a better plan." He grinned. A nasty grin I thought something, some screw had faltered in Mr. Rip Harper's structure.

"Come with me, boy."

I followed him through a narrow path leading into the rear of the garden. He led me to a small house where he kept a huge bulldog of incredible ugliness. My spirit fell. What was he going to do with me?

"Now boy, I am going to count to ten and you are going to climb up that mango tree. Then I am going to let Lizzie here keep vigil over you. If you try to escape she is going to tear you to bits, ha."

"But..." I tried to protest, but he interrupted.

"One... two... three..." I was already up the tree.

He went off without saying anything else. I think I cried a bit. The night was pitch dark now. Below I was just able to discern the form of the horrible monster. Then a swarm of mosquitoes came along and made life so miserable that I wished Rip Harper had given me a good walloping and sent me home. It was there in the darkness, that I decided that I was going to do something to Rip Harper. Something that would hurt him as much as he was hurting me.

A moon had come up and maybe I had drowsed off a bit between those branches because I had lost track of time when I heard a voice below calling. "All right, come down, boy."

I climbed down.

"Maybe I am getting a bit soft here," he touched his chest above his heart. "I am going to give you a chance, boy, ha. But let me warn you that if you loose your foolish head and come back here again I am going to skin your hide, understand?"

I was far too angry with Rip Harper to make any reply. I just walked out of his garden. At the gate he told me that I could have climbed down that tree and walked out of the garden and Lizzie wouldn't have done a thing, except maybe lick my hands.

I walked away that morning with deep bitterness, filled with a feeling of revenge so strong that I could almost taste it in my mouth. If there were any possibility of obtaining a gun, I would have returned, called out Mr. Harper and killed him.

At home my brother was very apologetic, saying that he had just had time to escape himself and had he made any attempt to warn me, both of us would have been caught. Ches Burns had fallen ill suddenly and the weekly poker game was postponed. Thus the reason for Rip Harper's unexpected return home.

It could be detrimental to both man's mental and physical status if his pride is injured. More so, if his pride is in himself, his ability and his notoriety. The plan which I had conceived to even my score with Rip Harper was one that could injure his pride deeply. He might never be the same man again if I succeeded. But, I rationalized, "Tit for tat." So, having come to the appointed time and place, I hid myself and waited for our Mr. Harper.

He came to the pond at five o'clock as usual, stripped off every stitch of his clothing and plunged himself into the cold black water. When he had swam out into the centre of the pond, I came out and took up all his clothes, with the exception of his boots and shouted after him.

"How'd you like to walk through Dove Head naked, Mr. Harper?"

"Hey! Put down those clothes at once," he bellowed after me.

"Why don't you come and get them." I replied.

He began to swim towards me. For a moment I thought of putting down his clothes and running to save my skin, then I remembered myself between those branches tortured by mosquitoes, his horrible monster keeping vigil under me, and his laughter at my discomfiture and those inseparable thoughts drove me onwards with his clothes, thinking not of the consequences which might have resulted from my actions, but of my satisfaction in seeing him hurt.

Getting into town otherwise than through the one narrow dirty street was impossible, more so in one's nakedness, since the whole area was infested with sickening thorn wisp known as 'tear-my-coat.' The people of Dove Head seldom visited that area and nobody save Rip Harper was ever known to swim in the pond which looked as if it were the home of horrible monsters. The water is very cold even at noon when the sun is hottest. The colour of the water is blackish brown. He was definitely not able to

linger in there for a very long while. He would have to stay
by the creek side and wait for me or walk through the town
nude. Either way I would have my revenge. I went home
and had supper.

Night came to Dove Head, and with it a swarm of mosquitoes as per usual. I relished the thought of Rip Harper's
misery as he was being tortured in his nakedness by those
disgusting little insects. I felt no pity. I returned to the spot,
where I had hidden his clothes, at eight o'clock, intending
to give him one more hour, just to even the score some
more, then give him his clothes. But only half an hour had
past when I heard approaching noises. From my ren-
dezvous I could see several lighted torches. That meant it
was a search party, which made my plans work out even
better than I had anticipated. They passed me and when the
last person went by I followed.

"Here are his shoes!" some one shouted.

"Rip Harper! Rip Harper! Yahooooo." Everybody shouted and shouted.

No reply.

"I see no clothes," a police officer remarked.

"Maybe he caught a sudden heart attack and fell into the
pond," another suggested.

They searched the entire area and found no sign of Mr.
Rip Harper. Joan and Sylvia were weeping mornfully. I felt
sorry for them. If their father had really drown I was the
one responsible. Suppose the police would find out I was
the one who hid his clothes, forcing him to remain in the
cold water, thereby catching a cramp which resulted in his
death? Surely I would be the one who would be arrested
and charged with his murder. They searched along the
creek side almost from one corner to the other.

They took sticks and pushed it into the water where it

was assumed he would have fallen from and got no result. Two hours the search continued fruitlessly.

"It's hopeless," the police office said mopping his head with a damp handkerchief. "If he is down there, there is very little we can do. We must return tomorrow with a dory and some divers to get him up... Okay you boys over there, call it off for the night."

Sylvia and Joanie became hysterical. Someone from the crowd came forward and assisted. They were led away crying hysterically. I wanted to go and help Sylvia, but I felt unclean to touch her, being her father's murderer.

"Rip Harper was a good man." Someone from the crowd remarked.

The word 'was' sent around and a shiver of fear and realization went through me. Realization that Rip Harper was dead and that I, Bernard Madison, was his murderer. Why did I do such a foolish thing?

In misery and anguish I followed the crowd. I kept calling myself a murderer. I murdered the father of the girl I loved. I thought the best course I could take would be to go and make a clean confession. Then I told myself that no one had seen me go to the pond. No one had seen me remove Rip Harper's clothes while he was bathing. Would there be a possibility that no one might suspect that I was in any way connected with his death? There were all possibilities.

In town I followed the crowd to Rip Harper's house where some women were waiting. Amongst them was my mother. I did not want to see her neither did I want to talk to anyone. I was in a confused state of mind and my tongue might make a slip and give myself away. So I kept at a distance. Then I decided to go back to the pond. Why, I did not know, but I guess that there is a truth in the saying that all criminals must return to the scene of their crime. On my way I stopped and picked up his clothes. Was he a criminal? If so what really was his motive for causing the death of Harper. Was it not merely an unfortunate circumstance? I sat at the edge of the pond crying silently. I looked down at his oversize shirt and trousers and my fears and anguish increased. I wanted to jump into the chilled water then and drowned myself. I got up slowly, cupped my mouth and called out his name.

"Rip Harper! Rip Harper! Rip Harper!"

No reply. So I tried again.

"Yahooooooo. Yahooooooo."

Still no reply.

I could feel the wet tear drops making an avenue towards my mouth. They tasted salt. What was I to do? How could I ever face Sylvia again, being her father's murderer? Oh my sweet Sylvia, never shall I taste your sweet lips, never shall I feel the nearness of your soft enticing body. Never again shall your smile fill my soul with joy. O foolish me.

I stayed by the side of the pond for a long time. Somewhere in the forests a whip-o-will called for its mate and got a reply. Everywhere there was the buzz of crickets. I was alone with the spirit of a deadman. I began to shiver and became frightened. Then I made up my mind to return to town, and go at once to my father. I would confess to him and he must be able to advise me what to do. I knew he would tell me to go to the police. I will do his will.

Then out of the darkness a large hand rested on my shoulder. I almost fainted.

"Ha, a murderer returning to the scene of his crime." he said.

"Oh Mr. Harper." I exclaimed. Never being so happy to see any one in my life.

"I should kill you boy. I should kill you for what you done me tonight," he said.

I could not see his expression in the darkness. I wish I could.

"But I won't harm you," he continued. "I am going to take you to the police." Now that he was alive, the superficial joy of seeing him was gone and I began to think about what would happen to me for my crime. I would be charged for mischievous act and could go to jail for sixty days. Sixty days and I would not be able to return to school.

He took up his clothes and began to put them on. His bigness did not make him clumsy. His movements were graceful and swift. When he bent to put on his trousers, his face came near mine and I caught a glimpse of the expression of his face. His brows were tightly knitted, his eyes wild and his teeth clenched. He was struggling. A battle with himself to restrain from doing me something violent.

"Come," he said when he was clothed.

I followed him into town in silence. I was tempted to make a dash and run away from him. But knowing his reputation as a hunter and the knowledge of the type of forests I would have to penetrate, I considered otherwise. At the edge of town he stopped.

"Sam Madison would lick you for this and the police would jail you. What made you do it boy, ha?"

I remained silent.

"Mad at me for what I did to you the other night, eh?" He asked. Still I made no reply. We remained silently for a while, then he burst out into laughter. I thought he was going mad. The vibration of his laughter seemed to shake the very ground on which I stood.

"Go home, Slim," he said. He called me Slim.

"But... But... Sir..."

"Go home boy," he said. He continued laughing. "Never have I seen such a neat one performed. Even in my anger you have won my respect, boy. You always even your score, ha?"

"I am sorry I did that to you, Sir."

"There is nothing to be sorry about, son. I did you a mean trick and you did one back to me, so we are even, ha."

"Well...s...ir, I guess we are." I replied.

"Shake." He offered me his hands. That steel clamp of a hand. I took it. "No hard feelings. But mention nothing to anybody about what happened tonight. I will cook up a story and you can come and visit my Sylvia anytime you want."

Rip Harper is dead now and I am married to Sylvia. He did not die from my act. I feel free to tell his story.

Biographies

Leo H. Bradley Sr (born in Caye Caulker, Belize, 1926) is a retired librarian and teacher with a keen interest in history. He lived for some years in Trinidad and the United Kingdom where he studied librarianship before becoming the first qualified Belizean librarian. He has served both as a government archivist and as Chief Librarian as well as a newspaper editor.

Zoila M. Ellis (born in Dangriga, Belize, 1957) is a practicing legal attorney based in Belize. She grew up in Belize's rural areas and studied law at the University of the West Indies before returning to Belize where she worked as a magistrate and crown council. She became the first director of the Belize Legal Aid Centre and is heavily involved in woman's organisations.

Evan X Hyde (born in Belize City, Belize, 1947) is a senator, publisher and writer as well as an outspoken protagonist for black affairs. He majored in English at the Dartmouth College in Hanover, New Hampshire. On his return to Belize he helped form the United Black Association for Development (UBAD) and became its second president in 1969. He is an accomplished author, poet, playwriter and essayist.

Lawrence G. Vernon (born in Belize City, Belize, 1937) is a librarian who studied in the United Kingdom and worked for many years in the Belize National Library Service before being appointed Chief Librarian. He is currently Library Director at the University College of Belize.

Evadne L. Wade-Garcia (born in Monkey River, Belize, 1950) is Director of the Geology and Petroleum Unit in the Ministry of Science, Technology and Transportation. She studied at the University of the West Indies, Jamaica and the University of Dundee, Scotland. She is a writer of both children's books and novels.

John Alexander Watler now lives in Los Angeles, USA where he has resided for some time. He was the driving force behind an earlier collection of short stories, *Among My Souvenirs*, which he co-authored with Leo Bradley and Lawrence Vernon. His later works often appeared in *Brukdown* and he is known for his epic poetry which focused on Belizean history.

Sir Colville Young (born in Belize City, Belize, 1932) became Belize's second Governor-General in November 1993. He was educated at the University of the West Indies and York University in the United Kingdom. Before his appointment as Governor-General he was a lecturer at the University College of Belize where he served as founding president. He is a prolific author, composer, playwright and poet.

Michael D. Phillips made his first visit to Belize in 1982 and has been back many times since. What began as an innocent interest has become a passion, both personal and academic. He has presented his research on Belize at the SPEAR conference, 'Latin American Studies Association Convention Interdisciplinary Belize Conference' (1992) and at several smaller regional meetings. He has written extensively about tourism in Belize and recently published an article on that subject in *Belizean Studies*. Professor Phillips currently teaches in the Department of Humanities, Classics, and Comparative Literature at Brigham Young University in Provo, Utah where he is working on a history of the Festival of Arts as part of a larger work concerned with Nationalism and Cultural Change in Belize. Previous to his work at Brigham Young University Professor Phillips was a graduate student at the University of Chicago where he organized a workshop on Belize which included the participation of Zee Edgell and Robert Reneau. With a background in cultural studies, Professor Phillips is committed to the collection and preservation of the best of Belizean Arts and Letters. This collection is the first in a planned series.